Lucille of the Amish

Eliza Baker

Published by Trellis Publishing, 2021.

This is a work of fiction. Similarities to real people, places, or events are entirely coincidental.

LUCILLE OF THE AMISH

First edition. July 4, 2021.

Copyright © 2021 Eliza Baker.

ISBN: 979-8224866038

Written by Eliza Baker.

LUCILLE OF THE AMISH

ELIZA BAKER

Chapter One:

"So you are saying that you want me to marry a man that I don't even know?" Lucille knotted her hands together under her apron on her lap. To quell the anger rising in her chest, she dug her thumb nail into the soft skin between her fingers. Her mind was racing, and she knew that she could only stall for so long before her daed pressed her for an answer.

"Well, you'll get to know him before the wedding," her daed said as if that made any of it better.

"He's a very nice man," her maemm added.

Lucille's stomach flipped, and she could feel bile rising in her throat. So many words of anger pressed against the back of her throat, choking her with rage. But she knew that she could never say any of them to her parents. That wasn't how she had been raised. She had been taught from the time she was young to respect her elders, and do as she was told.

Taking a deep breath to calm herself, Lucille asked, "And what's his name?"

"Elliot King," her daed answered immediately. "He's thirty-four, and a widower. He has a little girl who is four. I believe her name is Naomi. Is that right, dear?"

"Actually I think his daughter's name is Natalie, and that she's three," Lucille's maemm said.

"Regardless, he'll be here this evening for dinner. The two of you can begin to get to know each other then," her daed said.

Lucille felt a wave of nausea wash over her, and she said, "I think I need to take a walk, get some fresh air, be alone for a bit."

Her parents exchanged a glance that Lucille couldn't quite read, but her maemm said, "That's a good idea, dear. Take your shawl. It's chilly out today."

Without waiting for her parents to say anything else, Lucille jumped up from her chair, and hurried out to the hallway where she snatched her shawl off the hook. The cold March air smacked her in the face, but didn't stop her. Lucille plunged into the outdoors sucking in fresh air until she felt like she could breathe again.

Once she was down the lane, out of site of the house, Lucille allowed the tears that had been gathering in the corners of her eyes to fall. How could her parents be doing this to her? Was she being punished for Rosemary's mistakes? She sniffed, and swiped at her cheeks.

Thinking about her older sister made her heart hurt. When Rosemary hadn't come back from her Rumspringa years, her parents had insisted that she be shunned. Lucille hadn't seen her sister in seven long years, unless she counted the handful of times they had run into each other in town.

Twenty-one didn't seem so old to Lucille. Why did her parents' think she needed help finding a husband? True, she didn't have a line of suitors knocking down their front door, but still, she didn't see how that made her unmarriageable.

The wind had picked up, whipping through the treetops, making a whistling noise. Lucille pulled her shawl tighter around her shoulders, and kept walking. She knew that now that she had agreed to her parent's plan, that things would move quickly. She was already a baptized member of the church, and presumably so was he since he had been married before and he had a child.

Lucille decided to cut through the woods to her cousin's farm. Sara would listen to her, commiserate with her. The two had been best friends since they were born, and Lucille knew that she could count on her cousin to give her sage advice. That, and cutting through the woods meant that if her daed came out looking for her, he'd have a harder time finding her. She would be the obedient daughter later, but right now she needed to sulk.

The woods were full of spring time bird song as Lucille trudged along the well worn path. Something stirred deep in her heart, and she knew from experience that it was a call to pray. She found a tree with a deep V in the trunk, and settled herself in.

Dear Lord, she prayed, *I thank you for all the blessings that you have bestowed upon me. I have more than I deserve, especially since I am a sinner. I ask that you forgive me my sins, and make my heart pure. I want to do your will, Lord, and I don't know why it is so hard for me to follow the path that you have laid out for me. Help me to be a better follower of you, Lord. Help me to submit to Your Will. Not what I want, but what you want. If it be Your Will, Lord, please let my parents see the foolishness of their plan for me. Help them see that it is what they want for me, not what You want for me. But only if it is Your Will. Amen.*

As she finished her prayer, Lucille wasn't sure she was satisfied or if she had prayed well. Still, she stood so that she could go the rest of the way to Sara's house. The sticks and leafy detritus crunched underfoot, and she frowned to herself. Had she been clear enough with the Lord? She had always been counselled in the verse from Matthew 7:7-8, which read, "[7]Ask, and it shall be given you; seek, and ye shall find; knock, and it shall be opened unto you: [8]For every one that asketh receiveth; and he that seeketh findeth; and to him that knocketh it shall be opened."

To Lucille, prayer was a way to connect with God, but also as a way to ask for things that she wanted...or in this case, didn't want. She had never really been sure if that was the right way to pray, but at that moment she didn't care because as she stepped out of the woods, she saw her daed getting down from his buggy. Lucille didn't hesitate as she turned on heel and ran back into the woods.

Chapter Two:

A twig snapped behind her, and Lucille turned abruptly to see her cousin trailing after her. Sara had a look on her face that made Lucille think that her daed had already gotten to say his piece. She sighed, and sank down onto a fallen log.

"Did he send you to find me?" Lucille asked as her cousin approached.

The sent of moss and damp earth filled the forest, and Lucille inhaled deeply. These woods had always been her safe place to run when she needed time alone, and the familiar smells calmed her a bit. Sara sat down next to her, and put an arm around Lucille's shoulder.

"Why didn't you tell me that this was what your parents' were thinking of doing?" Sara asked.

There was a slight accusatory tone in her voice, and Lucille couldn't blame her. Normally the two girls told each other everything. "I was as blindsided by this as you," Lucille said. "I had no idea they wanted to arrange a marriage for me."

"How can that be?" Sara asked. And silently, Lucille wondered the same thing. How could she have missed all the hints her parents had been giving her over the past months that they thought it was time for her to marry.

Sighing, Lucille shrugged her shoulders, moving them up and down in a full bodied shrug that did nothing to shake the heaviness away from her limbs and muscles. She felt like she was swimming, slogging her way through silty water, unable to get to the other side.

"I haven't been listening to them, I guess. When Maemm told me she thought it was time for me to find a husband, to settle down and have a family of my own, I guess I just thought that she meant I needed to socialize more, go to some sings. I don't know." Lucille shook her head, the anger she had felt earlier bubbling up in her chest again.

"And they never mentioned the possibility that they were going to find someone for you?" Sara asked, still seeming unable to wrap her head around what she was hearing.

Lucille heaved an impatient breath. "It's not that strange for there to be an arranged marriage in this community," she said, trying not to snap at her cousin. Lucille knew that the way she was feeling wasn't Sara's fault, and she didn't want to make her cousin take the brunt of her anger.

"I know," Sara said softly, "but it usually seems as if both of the parties have been widowed, and they are looking to make a life together after their tragedies."

"Elliot lost his wife," Lucille said, choking out the name of her fiancé. "I can't remember if my maemm and daed told me what happened or not. But I do remember that he has a little girl named Natalie."

Sara's eyes sprang wide. "You're going to be a mother just like that?"

"Just like that," Lucille echoed. The thought of marrying a complete stranger made her feel despondent, but she had to admit that the thought of being the step-mother to the stranger's little girl didn't make her feel that way at all. If anything, Lucille was even excited about that prospect. Not that she was going to admit that to Sara at the moment. No, at the moment she wanted to keep that thought to herself.

"Your daed is pretty upset that you ran off," Sara commented.

Lucille narrowed her eyes. "I didn't run off. He and Maemm knew that I wanted to take a walk to think about what they sprang on me."

Sara shrugged. "Well, regardless of what he knew or you think he knew, he wants you home right away. Your beau is coming over to meet you."

The teasing lilt in her cousin's voice fueled the anger that was already burning in her, and Lucille knew that if she didn't leave right at that moment, she would say something that she would regret. "I'll see you later," she said to her cousin through gritted teeth.

"Lucille, wait," Sara called after her cousin, but Lucille didn't turn around.

As Lucille walked, she fumed. How could her daed invade her walk like this? She had agreed to be home to meet Elliot whatever his name was. Hadn't she? Her anger flagged when she realized that she might not have agreed after all. She had been in such a hurry and her head had been so full of conflicting thoughts and emotions that she knew she hadn't been thinking clearly. Or listening well for that matter.

Climbing over a fallen tree branch, Lucille's skirt snagged on a twig, throwing her off balance. Her arms pinwheeled as she tried to regain her balance, but she pitched forward into a muddy stew of leaves.

With a groan, Lucille pushed herself into a sitting position. She was covered from head to toe in sticky goo. Her maemm would be furious with her, and she suspected that her daed would think she had gotten messy on purpose. Even though she wasn't a child any longer, they continued to treat her like one. And now she had to rush home so that she could clean up before her fiancé got there.

As she rushed through the woods toward the main road, Lucille did her best to wipe most of the mud off her face and out of her hair. *Dear Lord,* she prayed as she ran, *I know that it is presumptuous to ask for this, but please let this Elliot man call off the wedding. If he were to call it off, then I wouldn't have to be married, and Maemm and Daed could save face. I know it's selfish, but please don't let this ruin my life. I just know it will. Amen.*

Chapter Three:

Lucille had hoped that she could sneak into the house through the back door, and no one would notice. That wasn't the case, however, as her maemm caught her just as Lucille's foot had hit the first step.

The gasp was what stopped her, but she prayed that if she didn't have to turn around, then she wouldn't have to explain herself. "Lucille!" Maemm's voice was a mixture of shock and disapproval and disappointment. The last was the hardest for Lucille to deal with. She had always tried her hardest to be good and obedient, but certain times she chose the wrong path. This had clearly been one of those times.

"Yes, Maemm?" she asked. Holding her breath, Lucille squeezed her eyes shut as she waited for her mother's reply.

"Where have you been?" Maemm asked in a tone that left no question about what she thought.

"I just went to see Sara," Lucille said, trying to keep her voice even. She gripped the banister on the staircase with her left hand, and fingered her damp, muddy apron with her right. If she had to turn around, then she would be in more trouble than she was at the moment.

Maemm made a disapproving noise deep in her throat. "Go upstairs and freshen up," she said. "Elliot will be here soon, and I want you to make a good impression."

Feeling like a chastised child, Lucille hurried upstairs. Despite her resolve to let the goodness in her heart rise to the surface, she let her boots fall heavily on the wooden treads of the stairs, leaving no doubt what she thought about the whole arrangement.

After washing the mud off her hands and face in the wash basin in her room, Lucille quickly changed into her nicer dress. As she fastened the hooks at her waist and neck, she couldn't help but wonder a little about Elliot King. She was certain that they must have crossed paths at some point, but for the life of her she couldn't remember when that might have been. He was older than she was; a father and a widower. How as she going to get along with him? He knew so much more about the world than she did? Even in their relatively sheltered world, that meant something.

Being a mother, now that was something that Lucille had always dreamed about, and in her deepest heart she knew that even if it was happening sooner than she would have liked, she was more than okay with it.

Straightening her kapp, Lucille took one last look in the mirror, and sighed. She couldn't hide up here any longer. Her maemm and daed would want her in the front room when Elliot arrived. She wondered if he would be bringing his daughter with. Since her parents had just hatched this plan on her that morning, she had no idea what was going to happen now.

Her daed was nowhere to be seen, and Lucille was relieved. Despite the fact that Elliot would be there any moment, that didn't mean that her daed wouldn't yell at her for being gone so long earlier. Her maemm came over to her, and began fussing with Lucille's clothing, tucking stray hairs into her kapp and brushing imaginary wrinkles out of her apron.

"You look...nice," Maemm said finally.

Lucille ducked her head, biting her lip to hold in another sigh. "Danke," she said.

"Now, where can your daed be?" Lucille watched as her maemm bustled over to the curtain, peered out, and gasped. "Elliot King is coming up the driveway now. Lands' alive, where is your daed?"

"Is he out in the barn?" Lucille asked. "Did he have to put the horse away?"

"Of course," her maemm said. "I'll be right back in. You let Elliot King in, and offer him some refreshments. And be polite."

Lucille waited until she heard the back door shut before she let out another sigh. Just then, there was a knock on the front door. Steeling her nerves, Lucille brushed her hands over her apron to dry her suddenly sweaty palms, and hurried to great her...guest.

When she opened the door, the man who stood in front of her caught her off guard. He was taller than she had expected, taller than any of the men in her family. He swept the simple straw hat off his head with one hand, leaving his blond hair slightly askew as he offered her his other hand by way of greeting. As she took it, she noticed how the left side of his mouth hitched a little higher than the right side when he smiled, and his blue eyes crinkled kindly. Despite all of her reservations, she found herself thinking that he was quite handsome.

"You must be Lucille," he said. "I'm your fiancé, Elliot."

She wasn't sure if he meant the words as a joke or not, but as soon as he said the word "fiancé" all her anger from earlier in the day came rushing back. She dropped her hand and stepped back. "As far as I know, I haven't officially agreed to anything yet," she said. "I was under the impression that this was simply for us to meet one another so we can see if we're compatible."

Elliot grinned at her. "You need a husband, and I need a wife. What could be more compatible than that?" he asked.

She was just about to say something else, something that she would probably regret, when her parents came through the back door. They hurried through the kitchen and into the front room. "Ah, Elliot," her daed said. "I see the two of you are just meeting. Come in, come in. My wife and I were just talking, and we think that this weekend would indeed be a fine time for the wedding."

A buzzing sound started in Lucille's ears, and she was certain that she hadn't heard her daed correctly. When the moment passed, and she realized that they were all still talking about it, dread filled Lucille from top to toe, and she thought she might get sick to her stomach.

"Won't it be wonderful, Lucille?" her maemm asked.

Lucille couldn't do anything but nod, even as she felt her whole world collapsing around her.

Chapter Four:

The wedding had happened in a blur with a big dinner served afterward. If Lucille hadn't been so stressed out by the whole thing, she might have been able to admit that her maemm had given her everything she'd ever dreamed of.

Settling in to Elliot's house, settling in to being his wife, and settling in to being Natalie's maemm left Lucille drifting in a strange haze. She walked through each day, performing her chores and going through the motions of her daily life, but she never felt connected to Elliot or her new life. Natalie was a high spot, but even the little girl wasn't enough to make her believe that her new life was anything but a bad dream that she would wake from soon.

One morning, about a month after they had been married, Lucille took a deep breath, and said, "Would you mind terribly if I took a walk by myself after breakfast?"

Elliot looked at her with a relieved smile. Lucille wasn't sure what to make of the look, but she decided to let it go. Her maemm had always cautioned her to hold her tongue on her first reaction because Lucille often had the tendency to spit out whatever came into her head.

"Of course," he said. "I'll take Natalie out to the barn with me. It's been a while since she helped me with a milking."

Lucille chewed on her lower lip. Why did Elliot have to be so accommodating? She knew that she should be trying to learn to love him, but she still prayed daily for a way out of the marriage. She knew it was her own fault for agreeing to it, but by now she had convinced herself that she had been tricked into it. The more she told herself that, the more she believed it.

The second she stepped out the door, Lucille felt the constricting tension ease off of her shoulders. She hurried down the drive to the lane that ran in front of the house, and then after looking both ways, she crossed to the meadow beyond. A deer trail led down to a small stream, and after making her way along the banks for half a mile, she found her favorite place to rest, a large rock surrounded by reeds. No one would ever find her here.

Dear Lord, I don't know what I have done to be punished like this, but if you show me, I will promptly confess to the bishop in front of the whole community. It isn't that Elliot is a bad man. He's not, in fact, I know that he's nice and kind and gentle, but I didn't pick him. I'm angry, Lord, and I know that I shouldn't be. So, I suppose that should be sin number one. I just wish that I could turn back the clock, and make a different choice.

Lucille paused, and gazed out across the stream. Being here by herself calmed her. And when she had spilled out her prayers to God, she felt better, but also guiltier. She knew that she should trust the Lord's path for her, even if that path included being married to Elliot.

I know that I shouldn't ask you for this, Lord, but please let me find a way to get out of this marriage. Amen.

Glancing up at the sun, Lucille decided that she should be getting back. Despite the fact that she wasn't willing to accept her marriage, she still wanted to do her duty as a wife. The cooking and the cleaning and the caring for Natalie soothed her. It was at night when she went to bed alone (thankfully in her mind) or when Elliot came into the house and drew near her, that made her stomach jump.

As Lucille walked slowly back toward the house, she heard a faint yipping coming from down near the water. Pausing in the long reeds, she listened harder. Another yip. Lucille waded into the long grass, pausing now and then to listen to the sound.

Down by the water Lucille found a little puppy, curled on a rock, obviously weak from hunger. Without thinking twice, Lucille reached out and scooped the little animal into her arms. "You poor think," she cooed to the dog.

The puppy yipped softly at her, and then settled against her chest. Lucille didn't know what Elliot would say when she brought the little guy home, but she was determined to keep him. Besides he would make a good playmate for Natalie. Lucille had always had a dog at home, so she thought that maybe having a dog in the house would make her feel more at home at Elliot's. The thought made her stop in her tracks. Did she really just think that she wanted to feel at home at Elliot's house? Did she want that to be her home? No, of course not. She wanted to go home, to her real home, and get her life back on track.

By the time she got back to the farm, she was ready for an argument over the puppy. She was going to keep him no matter what. Besides she had already named him Kip. She climbed the stairs, and stepped into the cool of the house. "Hello?" she called.

"We're in the kitchen," Elliot called back.

"Look what I found down by the stream," Lucille said brightly.

"A puppy!" Natalie exclaimed.

"Aw, poor little guy," Elliot said. Then he took the puppy from her to get it cleaned up, Natalie following at his heels.

Lucille watched father and daughter as they walked to the sink, and she was annoyed as she felt her heart stir with warmth at Elliot's compassion. She didn't want to thaw toward him, because if that happened, then it was all a slippery slope from there.

Chapter Five:

Despite her desire for her life to have taken a different path, Lucille found herself indeed thawing toward her husband and toward her new situation. Natalie had smashed through the wall that Lucille had constructed, and was easy to love. Kip, the new puppy, proved easy to love as well. From his oversized paws and long floppy ears, Lucille and Elliot deduced that he was probably some kind of hound dog.

"Who could ever just abandon such a sweet little thing like this?" Lucille asked one night as they sat out on the front porch. Spring had turned into early summer, and she and Elliot had taken to sitting out on the porch after Natalie was in bed. Even though Lucille was settling into her new life, that hadn't stopped her from praying that somehow she could still go back to her old one. Though, now she was less and less sure of what that actually meant. What was the old life she was seeking to get back?

"I have no idea," Elliot said. "But he sure is lucky that you found him. When that late winter storm blew in, he would have been a goner."

Lucille nodded, shivering at the thought. She had never had a dog that she loved as much as Kip. She knew that God had given him to her so that she could start seeing herself as part of this family unit. Not that she saw herself as that yet, not by a long shot. Still, she could see that Kip was the glue that was slowing adhering them all together.

Elliot coughed. He thumped his chest with his fist, and then coughed again. Lucille frowned at him. "Are you feeling okay?" she asked. When he coughed in response, she noticed a deep rattling for the first time.

"Just an irritated throat," Elliot replied, giving her a weak smile. His voice was scratchy and hoarse. How had she not noticed he was feeling bad before that moment?

"You should get on up to bed," Lucille said with a firmness that surprised her. "I'll go and fetch the doctor."

"I'm not feeling that poorly," he protested. "Besides there are all kinds of chores that need to be done."

"I'll go get one of my brothers," Lucille said as she waved off his concerns.

Reluctantly Elliot stood. Lucille felt a flash of determination at the doubtful look on his face. "Come on," she said, standing as well. She reached out to take his hand, a gesture that surprised both of them, and was startled further to feel how hot his skin was. "You're burning up!"

"I'm fine," Elliot grumbled, but it was becoming clearer and clearer that he was anything but fine.

"We're going to make sure that you are," Lucille agreed even as a degree of guilt crept in. She had been praying so hard for there to be a way for this marriage to be over...she hadn't meant that she wanted Elliot to get sick. The Lord had known that, hadn't he?

Swallowing hard, Lucille called, "Natty? We're going to go out for a little bit. Grab your shawl."

"Let me at least hitch up the horse to the buggy," Elliot said before another fit of coughing overwhelmed him, and he doubled over.

"No," Lucille said. "I know how to hitch up a buggy. You go get to bed. I'll take care of the rest."

Natalie obediently fetched her shawl, and Lucille lifted her into her arms. Taking a deep breath she opened the door, and was relieved to find the spring day warm with only a slight chill in the breeze. "Where are we going?" Natalie asked softly.

"To see my maemm and daed," Lucille replied as she crossed the yard toward the barn where the buggy stood waiting for them.

"Grossmammi and grossdaddi?" Natalie asked.

"Yes, exactly. Grossmammi and grossdaddi," Lucille repeated, hugging the little girl tighter.

After Lucille set Natalie on a little bench in the corner of the barn, she set about hooking the horse up to the hitch. When she and Natalie were in the buggy, she flicked the reins and expertly steered the horse out of the barn. She realized that Elliot had no reason to think that she could do anything for herself because in all the time she had lived with him as his wife she hadn't done much for herself besides cook and clean. Why did it have to take something like Elliot getting sick for her to see how much more she could have done around the farm? She had loved helping at home. Now this was her home, and she was going to have to start acting like it.

"Now, we have to hurry," Lucille said, more to herself than to Natalie.

The little girl just smiled up at her as Lucille urged the horse into a brisk trot, trusting that her new maemm would take care of everything. When Lucille saw the trust in the little girl's eyes, the guilt of what Lucille had been praying for all these weeks walloped her upside the head. If only she had approached the whole situation with an open heart like the good Lord always asked her to, then perhaps she would have seen this trouble coming.

By the time she pulled into her parents' driveway, Lucille had already prayed for forgiveness multiple times, and she had come up with a rough plan of action. Both of her parents came out onto the porch followed by a few of her siblings. From the quizzical looks on their faces, she knew that she needed to start talking fast.

Jumping down from the buggy, she pulled Natalie into her arms. Striding up the porch steps, she said, "Elliot is ill. I think it might be pneumonia, but I need to get the doctor. We also need help at the farm. I've prayed about this, and now I need to know if you will help me? Us?"

Chapter Six:

Of course her parents said yes right away, but Lucille couldn't help but feel relieved. After the way she had acted—like a spoiled brat of a child, rather than a grown woman—she had harbored some fear that her parents might hold a grudge against her. But they did not as she should have known, and indeed they seemed glad to be invited into her life to help.

As soon as the plea had left her lips, both her parents jumped into action. Her maemm had taken Natalie, and told the other children to take the little girl inside. "I'll keep her here for the rest of the day so you can attend to the things you need to do," her maemm had said.

Lucille's daed had told her to head back home to Elliot. "I'll go fetch the doctor, and go around to your brother, Lars' farm to see if he can come help me with Elliot's milking and such," her daed had promised.

As Lucille drove back home, she prayed, *"Dear Lord, I know that I have already asked you to forgive me, but I must ask it again. I have been a terrible sinner, a terrible wife, and a terrible person. I should have trusted that your path would lead me somewhere better. Please let Elliot get better. Amen."*

When she entered the house, she was amazed at how quiet and still it felt, and a jolt of fear ran through her. Kip appeared suddenly by her side, and yipped. He then pulled on the hem of her skirt, leading her to the staircase. Climbing the stairs two at a time, she called, "Elliot?"

She found him lying on the floor just a few feet from the bed. "Elliot!" Lucille knelt down next to him, and was relieved to feel that he was breathing. A second later, he blinked up at her with a confused expression on his weary face. She reached out to brush his hair away from his forehead, and gasped when she realized that he was burning up with fever.

"I'm so sorry, Lucille," Elliot mumbled. "I know this isn't the life that you wanted."

"Stop that," Lucille said softly. "I should apologize to you. No, I do apologize to you, Elliot. I'm sorry for acting like a petulant child. You're right that I didn't want an arranged marriage. I said yes because I thought it was my duty to obey my parents, and I was angry about it. I never even gave you a chance."

"I don't know if you can, but I hope you can give us a chance," Elliot said. "I think that we could learn to love each other. I know that I already have feelings stirring toward you."

Lucille blushed. No one had ever spoken to her like this before. "I believe I have feelings stirring toward you too," she said. "And I'm not going anywhere. We're married, and my commitment is to you and Natalie and any more children who might come along."

Elliot gave her a look of surprise that would have been hard to miss even if she didn't think he was slightly delirious from his fever. "Our family," was all he said.

"Yes, our family," Lucille agreed. Then, tucking her arms under his, she helped him sit up. "We need to get you into bed now before the doctor arrives. And before you say anything else, my daed and Lars are going to help with the chores around here until you are on your feet again."

Elliot made a noise of protest, but when it became clear that he wasn't going to be able to do much on his own, he let Lucille help him into bed. As she pulled the covers up to his chin, he surprised her by catching her hand, and saying, "Thank you."

Her tongue was tied and stuck to the roof of her mouth. All she could manage was a soft reply before Kip let out a delighted yelp, and launched himself onto the bed. Lucille couldn't help but giggle, and even Elliot had to smile.

The doctor diagnosed pneumonia just as Lucille had thought, and after the first night, Lucille fetched Natalie. Together, the two of them made sure that Elliot got plenty of rest with Natalie entertaining him so that he wouldn't get bored while on bed rest. And while her daed certainly provided her a lot of help and support, Lucille surprised herself by insisting that she take over most of the farm work. "It's my home," she told her daed. "I want to make sure things run smoothly.

One balmy May evening after Natalie was in bed, Lucille brought two mugs of tea out to the front porch where Elliot was sitting watching the sun set. "Thank you," he said as she sat down beside him.

"It's just tea," she said with a smile. Now that she was one hundred percent committed to her new life she felt a lightness that she had never felt before in her life. It felt a lot like happiness.

Elliot gave her a serious look. "You know what I mean," he said. "Thank you for all of this. You've done an amazing job."

Lucille flushed. "You're welcome," she said. "But it's my home too. And I'll do whatever is needed here."

The two lapsed into a thick silence for some time before Lucille said, "I never thought that I would get past my own vision for my life, but now that I'm following God's path for me, things have never looked more beautiful. I can't tell you how much I love it here now."

"You have no idea how happy that makes me to hear you say that," Elliot said.

And then he leaned over to kiss her.

AMISH UNVEILED

SABRINA VICKS

Chapter 1: A Fresh Start

Sarah reached for her bonnet which had dropped from her bed to the floor during her restless sleep. She couldn't remember her dreams once she woke up, but the feeling of dread which accompanied her was slow to move from her body. She sat on the edge of the bed and studied the wall of her room carefully. It was an empty wall, no pictures to adorn it. No posters hung to cover up the holes left by angry fists.

She stood up from her bed and a wave of dizziness overtook her and she had to sit back down for fear of fainting. Inhaling deeply, she lifted herself once more from the bed and steadied herself against the wall. She had been like this for over week, but she refused to call in the doctor for a consultation.

Walking into the kitchen of her new home, she began preparing her breakfast—a simple meal of bread and porridge. She nibbled it thoughtfully as she considered what she might do this morning. It was Monday, so she would not be going into town to sell her quilts. She decided to take a walk along the riverside and explore her new community.

As she made her way down the steps of her house, she heard someone calling out her name. Sarah looked up and saw a young woman running up to her with an older woman in tow.

"Sarah!" the young girl called out. "Oh, I am so glad to finally meet you. I have been trying to introduce myself to you properly since you moved here, but I can never seem to find you at home. I'm Rebecca." The young girl smiled at her warmly and Sarah walked down the last step and extended her hand out to the women. Rebecca took it in hers and smiled as they shook.

"Hello, Sarah," the older woman said, having finally caught up with Rebecca. "My name is Esther. This is my daughter, Rebecca, although I'm afraid you have already learned that information."

Sarah smiled at the pair of them and said, "I am glad to meet both of you. I am sorry for the trouble you have had trying to introduce yourselves! I work often in the markets as I sell my quilts and when I am not there, well, usually I am taking a walk and getting fresh air."

"You mean to say that you go into town to sell your quilts?" Rebecca asked, shocked by Sarah's admission.

"Yes," Sarah nodded. "It seems peculiar, but it is much more lucrative and as I live by myself, I have only myself to rely on."

Sarah saw Rebecca and Esther share a knowing look and Sarah's own smile seemed to slide from her face. This community had been open to her and welcomed her in with open arms, but they still held to certain standards that Sarah knew she would never fulfill. She knew that to them, she was an unmarried woman who traveled into town by herself to make money. The idea sounded entirely too progressive, but Sarah also knew that she would never have it any other way. She had lived another life fulfilling the expectations of others and all it had brought her was misery.

"Well, I do suppose we should be heading back home," Esther said finally once the silence had breached dangerously on the side of being uncomfortable. Sarah nodded and the two women quickly retreated down the path from where they had come from. Sarah saw Rebecca glance furtively back in her direction before quickly turning her around.

Sarah began her walk much as she did every morning since she had arrived in this town. The river beside her bubbled up and triumphed over the smallest obstacles which stood in its way. Every pebble and branch it overcame, she could hear the rejoice in its movement. Sarah sat down beneath a tree and bowed her head in prayer.

She gave thanks to the Lord for all the guidance He had offered her in her life. She prayed to Him to show her kindness and to allow her to live peacefully in her new community. She wanted only to live as simply as possible and she swore to devote herself to Him fully.

"And please, Lord," Sarah whispered quietly, "watch over Jacob and show him the same love and mercy that you have always shown me."

She looked up and saw a small rabbit in the distance, his ears perking up as though he heard her prayer. She smiled to herself as she thought about the wonder of God and how one could find Him in everything they saw.

Sarah continued her walk and before she knew it, she had reached the end of the community. She was about to turn back the same path which she had come, but in a curious moment of spontaneity, she decided to try a new path.

She walked through the fields which lay on the border of the community and she admired the crops which they were growing. It had been a successful year and Sarah could tell that the harvest was nearly upon them. Walking without a definitive purpose, Sarah lost herself in reverie.

She began the day dream peacefully as she imagined a young boy running through the fields crying out in glee. She heard herself calling out to him, "Jacob! Jacob!" He turned and his piercing blue eyes touched her soul. The sky turned dark and all too quickly, rain began to pour from the heavens above. Sarah ran to Jacob and grabbed him by the hand, pulling him through the field. They ran all the way to their home where they stood in the doorway, dripping wet. Sarah looked at Jacob who was still wearing a joyful smile—he had thought their race through the field a game and begged her to go outside again. But she had to refuse him and as much as she hated to see the disappointment on his face, she dreaded something else much more. Sarah ushered Jacob to his room so that he could change into dry clothing, but the petulant child refused to budge as a protest. Just as she reached for him, the front door swung open and his father stepped inside. Jacob ran into his mother's arm. The man stared at them closely and after a moment, he shut the door behind him with a loud bang.

Sarah was pulled from her reverie as she ran into something. No, not something—someone.

"Oh, I am so sorry," she apologized as she took several steps backward. "I was not looking where I was going." She looked up and saw a man standing before her. He wore a small smile and his soft brown eyes gleamed. Sarah could not bring herself to utter another word.

"It happens to me all the time," the man said. "I'm Luke. It's nice to meet you. You must be Sarah?"

"Ye—yes," she stuttered. "How did you know?"

"My sister, Rebecca, has been going on and on about meeting you. She makes it a point to introduce herself to any new members of our community so that you don't feel alone here."

Sarah managed a small smile as she recalled her brief exchange with Rebecca from the morning. "I met your mother as well then, Esther."

"Yes, it is not often that you will find one without the other," he laughed. Sarah studied him carefully—the soft curve of his face, his slightly tanned skin which was shaded by his hat, the striking nose which would have seemed ridiculous on any other face, but for him, it seemed perfectly suitable.

"I should be going," Sarah muttered. She was growing wary of their exchange and although he had been merely kind to her, she knew that all too often, kindness from others came with a price.

Luke nodded at her briefly before returning to his work. Sarah dared one final glance at him as he navigated his fields knowingly and then walked the rest of the way home in a hurry. She closed the door behind her and exhaled a breath she hadn't even realized she'd been holding.

Sarah spent the remainder of the day working on a new quilt which she hoped to bring into the market to sell by this week. She toiled away, focusing on each stitch and expertly handled the needles. This was a form of prayer for her as well as she strongly believed that God worked through her hands and with Him as her guidance, they created beautiful works of art.

She put down her newest quilt and walked to the space where she stored all her quilts. From the lowest shelf, she pulled out a small blue quilt which she had made. She brushed her fingers gently over the small white letters which spelled the name Jacob. Closing her eyes, she brought the quilt up to her face and inhaled. It still smelled like him, a familiar scent of grass and boyhood. She thanked the Lord once again for allowing her to experience true joy with Jacob, even if it was ever so brief.

Sarah replaced the quilt on its shelf and closed the door. She walked into her bedroom and after removing her shoes and bonnet, she laid down in her bed and closed her eyes. She willed herself to sleep a dreamless sleep, but alas, like waves on the ocean, dreams came crashing down upon her and she could only pray that the Lord would not let her drown before she awoke.

Chapter 2: The Marketplace

Sarah awoke the next morning just as the sun peeked her head over the horizon. As she moved about the house, preparing for her day at the marketplace, the light slowly spilled in, bathing her in the glorious colors which had always inspired her. She stopped for a moment and whispered a thank you to the Lord.

Sarah had always been a pious woman—she believed strongly in the power of her faith and she knew with certainty, that the Lord had a plan for her. She struggled, however, when it came to others. It was not that she believed that the Lord cared for her more than others or that she was in any way more important, she just believed that in this life, people would act against God more often than not. They would reject His plan for their lives and they would try to bring down those around them as well.

This plagued her as she set up her stand in the marketplace. Many offered her assistance, but she refused any help, determined to succeed only with the help of the Lord. She found herself standing in the marketplace with most of her quilts spread out when a sudden rush of dizziness hit her once again. She swayed to the side and tried to place her hand against the station to steady herself, but she caught hold of a quilt and they began to fall together.

Someone caught her by the arms just as she was about to hit the floor. She squeezed her eyes shut and then opened them as the person lifted her to her feet. She turned and came face to face with Luke.

"I see you have a tendency to fall into me," he said with a laugh.

Sarah blushed furiously at his attempt at humor and she took a few cautious steps back. Luke studied her curiously and then asked, "Are you alright, Sarah? You do not look so well."

"Yes, I am fine. Thank you," Sarah said, still struggling to fully recover. Luke bent down to pick up the quilt which had fallen to the floor, but Sarah rushed over and plucked it from his hands. "It is okay, I can set it back in its place."

Luke watched her with a serious expression and it struck Sarah how handsome he was even when he was not smiling. She bent down to pick up the last two quilts and laid them out in their places.

"Did you make all of these?" Luke asked.

"Yes," Sarah smiled as she examined her work. "I started when I was very young and it grew from a hobby to a means of living." Luke smiled at her as she spoke and he was truly overcome with admiration for her beautiful creations.

"I would like to buy one for my mother," he said.

Sarah looked at him with a wary expression. She did not know whether he was sincerely interested in purchasing one of her quilts or if this was some sort of test to prove that she should not be in the market.

"I have a new one I have started," Sarah said slowly. "Once I finish it, I should give it to you as a gift."

"A gift?" Luke asked, unsure of how to interpret her actions. "For what?"

"For helping me today," Sarah smiled and this seemed to put Luke at ease. He nodded and looked over her quilts one final time before he started moving away. Sarah was reluctant to let him go, although she did not know why. "Why are you in the market today?"

Luke turned around and walked back towards her. He opened the satchel which he wore around him and inside, she could see a variety of fresh vegetables which he had picked from his garden.

"I come to the market sometimes when we have a bountiful harvest to sell the surplus food," he explained. "It helps us to buy what we need for the next year." Sarah nodded as she admired the ripe tomato which sat on the top. Luke seemed to pick up on her interest as he pulled that specific tomato from the bag and handed it to her.

"What is this for?" she asked, holding the tomato in her hand.

"It is a gift," Luke smiled. "For falling into me today. Again." He let out a small laugh and Sarah couldn't help but laugh with him. Luke turned from her and walked over to his own booth down the way where he set up all the vegetables on display.

Soon the market was bustling with people and Sarah had many people approaching her and inquiring about the quilts. However, whenever they asked the price, they often frowned at her response and walked away. Was she really asking too much for these handmade quilts?

Another gentleman approached her booth and she observed him from a distance. He wore a simple suit with a red tie and expensive looking shoes. In between his mouth and nose, there was a silly looking mustache. Sarah had always wondered why men should want to grow only mustaches instead of full beards. What was the purpose of them anyway?

His question pulled her away from her thoughts and she asked, "I'm sorry, what did you ask?"

He looked slightly annoyed at the idea of repeating himself, so he spoke slowly to ensure that she would hear every word. "I asked you if these were handmade?"

Sarah nodded and said, "Yes, I have made all of these." The man nodded appreciatively and placed his hand under his chin as he stroked his mustache in thought.

"How much for this one?" he asked. He held up one of her most recent quilts—it was a beautiful patchwork quilt with soft blues and white. It had been inspired by the clouds in the sky and if one looked very carefully at the center piece, there was a small hand.

"This quilt is $350," Sarah said with a small nod. The man looked at her over the quilt and lowered it slowly back to its place on the table.

"I see," he said. "Well, thank you for your time."

Sarah watched as he stepped away from the table and quickly she asked, "How much would you offer for it?" The man stopped walking. He looked from her to the quilt and back to her again.

"I will give you $50 for it," he said. He pulled out his wallet from his pocket and handed her a $50 bill. Sarah did not fail to notice the plethora of other bills he had as well, but she took the money from him and the man smiled at her as she folded the quilt for him and handed it over.

"Thank you," Sarah said quietly.

"No, thank you!" The man walked away and Sarah stared after him. She had spent over $50 just on the materials needed to make that quilt. At this rate, she would never be able to sustain herself. The bustle slowed down and the experience with the man had drained Sarah. She began wrapping up her booth and storing her quilts away.

"How did you do?" Sarah looked up and saw Luke standing there, that familiar smile holding on.

"I did not do well," she said quietly. Luke walked over to her and began helping her fold the quilts. Sarah looked up at him and said, "I really do not need help. I have been doing this by myself for a long time."

Luke nodded, not letting go of the quilt in his hands. "I know you do not need my help, but I am offering it to you anyway. Just because you have been doing something the same way for so long, does not mean you are incapable of change."

Sarah stopped folding and glanced at the man standing before her. She could not help but feel a sort of goodness about him. She did not reply to him, she merely nodded, and the two of them worked together to pack up her quilts. They walked together outside where Luke offered her a ride in his carriage.

Climbing aboard the carriage with her quilts, Sarah felt a sense of calm come over her. Luke climbed up next to her and took the reins in hand and the two of them rode along in a comfortable silence. They could talk about their lives and the world, they could discuss the Lord, and yet, they chose silence. For most, this might suggest a sort of incompatibility, but for Sarah, she started to feel that maybe Luke understood her better than she understood herself.

He dropped her at her house and helped her carry in all of the quilts. Tilting his hat to her, they said their farewells and Sarah sat down, replaying the day she'd had. She picked up her newest quilt and with a renewed determination, she set to finishing it that night.

As she laid down that night, she felt extremely grateful. She thanked the Lord for leading her to this community and for allowing her to find a friend in Luke. She thanked him for helping her sell the quilt in the market. And finally, she asked him to watch over Jacob.

Sarah closed her eyes and drifted off into a deep slumber. She dreamed of the day that Jacob and she ran together through the field in the rain. She held her child in her arms, but this time when the door opened and a man stepped inside, it was Luke standing before them.

Chapter 3: The Doctor

The day began much the same as every other day and Sarah found a sweet comfort in the routine. She rarely acted outside of her schedule, but sometimes a peculiar mood would come over her which would prompt her to do exactly that. She decided not to go to the market on this day and instead, she walked over to Luke's house carrying the new quilt.

She knocked on the door softly and Luke pulled it open. As soon as his eyes landed on her, he blessed her with his sweet smile. She nodded at him and said hello.

She held out the quilt to him and said, "As promised. My gift for you."

Luke took the quilt and opened it, admiring the beautiful colors she had arranged together. "It is beautiful," he said. "My mother will love this. Come in, come in." He pulled the door open and Sarah walked inside, unsure of what she might find.

Rebecca peered at her from behind a wall and Sarah waved at her.

"Sarah!" Rebecca exclaimed, as though they were old friends who had not seen each other in lifetimes. "I am so glad you could find time to stop by. But wait, I thought you work at the markets on these days?"

Sarah nodded and said, "Yes, I usually do. But today, I decided to stay here."

"Well, we are glad you did," Rebecca smiled. Sarah could not determine whether Rebecca's joy was sincere or whether it was manufactured for the sake of her brother. "Esther!" Rebecca called. "You must come see who has visited us!"

Sarah looked at Luke who shook his head at his sister and laughed. Rebecca smiled at him and then her eyes flickered to the wall where she had just emerged. Esther came out from behind the wall and immediately smiled at Sarah when she saw her.

"Oh, Sarah. How wonderful to see you again," Esther said.

"Look, mother. She has made you this quilt." Luke handed his mother the new quilt and she took it and unfolded it. Both women let out small gasps as they looked it over, admiring every detail.

"It's beautiful," Esther said. "Thank you very much for this." Sarah smiled at the two women and looked again at Luke who was wearing a curious expression. "I have a wonderful idea," Esther said suddenly.

"Luke, why don't you take Sarah for a walk today? I know she quite enjoys walking along the river, don't you?"

Sarah nodded at this sentiment and considered the idea of having Luke accompany her. To her surprise, his company actually sounded like a wonderful plan.

"Yes, I think that's what we will do," Luke said. He took Sarah's elbow and led her towards the door. Sarah shivered at his touch and Luke let go reflexively, misinterpreting her reaction.

The two women stood in the doorway and waved at them as they walked down the path together. Sarah looked up at Luke and asked, "What is it?"

"Those two have been trying to get me to ask you on a walk since you moved here," Luke laughed. "They are relentless. I told them that you would need time to adjust to your new surroundings and to get your bearings, but once you ran into me in the fields, well. Let's just say I was waiting for the right moment."

Sarah felt a warmth spread through her, touching every piece of her heart which she had thought she had hidden away, never to be seen again. She recalled the meeting between herself and Rebecca and Esther and the thought dawned on her that perhaps the two of them had not been passing judgements of her, but they were trying to gauge her character for Luke.

The two of them walked along the river and talked with each other amiably. "Your sister and mother both seem very nice," Sarah observed. "Does your father also live there?"

Luke shook his head. "No, my father passed away just before Rebecca was born."

Sarah nodded. "My mother passed when I was young," Sarah explained. "She was giving birth to my younger sister, but there were complications and neither of them survived."

Luke listened to her as she spoke and nodded his head thoughtfully. "It is curious at times when we ponder why loved ones are taken from us. We know that it is all in the Lord's plan, we know that whatever He has planned for us includes learning to grow from these experiences. But still, one does wonder for a reason sometimes."

Sarah shook her head. "No, I trust in His plan fully. I will not wonder for something which He does not desire me to know."

Luke observed her and said, "I admire the strength of your faith. I must admit that sometimes I express myself a little too freely, even to those who I do not know very well."

"You shouldn't take what I said as a judgment against your own character," Sarah explained. "I have just been through many trials and the only way I have survived it all was with His strength and guidance."

Luke considered her words carefully and Sarah could tell that he was debating whether to ask about her trials. In the end, he did not push her for more information and Sarah was relieved that she could keep her secret safe with her.

They sat beneath the tree by the river and spoke of the community and the people here. Luke told her that she would make many friends here who would always be more than willing to help her if she ever needed to ask. Sarah could feel him chipping away steadily at the insecurity which had grown within her, the wariness of others, especially of men.

She talked with him about her old community, the families there lived much to themselves. They were taught to lend a helping hand to others, but it seemed as though everyone hesitated when they saw that someone was in trouble.

"Is that why you left?" Luke asked her.

"In part," Sarah replied slowly. The moment had come—would she tell him the truth of her past which haunted her dreams? Could she trust this fragile friendship to withstand such a blow? Sarah looked at Luke and decided that while he might be able to handle the truth, she was not yet ready to deliver it.

"It is getting late," Luke said, realizing that Sarah had grown distant. "We should get back." Sarah nodded and stood from her place beneath the trees. As soon as she stood up, the dizziness came crashing down upon her with such force that her vision grew black and she fainted into Luke's arms.

Luke carried her from the river all the way to the doctor's house. He knocked on the door loudly and the doctor pulled it open, surprised at the scene before him. He ushered Luke inside and instructed him to lie her down on the table. As the doctor gathered some towels, Luke heard Sarah mumbling something. He leaned forward and listened carefully as she mumbled, "Jacob, no. Please, not Jacob."

The doctor gently pushed Luke back from his position and instructed him to wait in the other room while the doctor completed his examination. The doctor opened each one of Sarah's eyelids and studied her eyes with a magnification tool and flashlight. He pressed gently on her stomach and as he was doing this, Sarah stirred.

She looked around the room, but before panic could seize her, the doctor walked up and smiled down at her. "I am the doctor," he said calmly. "It seems that you had fainted while out with Luke today and he brought you in to see me. Can you sit up?"

Sarah nodded and climbed down from the table and sat in one of the chairs. She looked at the doctor as he studied her carefully.

"You are Sarah, is that correct? You recently joined our community." Sarah nodded and the doctor smiled at her. "Well, it's nice to meet you, although it may have been nicer under different circumstances."

Sarah managed a weak laugh and then coughed. "Is there something wrong with me?" she whispered to him. "This is not the first time I have been dizzy, although it is the only time I have fainted."

"Sarah, may I ask a question which you may find difficult to answer? Please know that I am only trying to gather more information to help you."

Sarah nodded.

"Were you married in your previous community?"

Sarah was shocked by his question—she knew that he had stated it would be difficult to answer, not impossible. She opened her mouth to speak, but no words came out. The doctor waited patiently for her to recover herself.

Finally, Sarah nodded and said, "Yes."

The doctor looked at her matter-of-factly and said to her, "And the man, he was violent towards you?"

Tears sprang to Sarah's eyes as her walls came crashing down around her. This poor doctor, meeting her for the first time and yet able to identify all of her deepest and darkest secrets.

"You don't need to respond to that, Sarah. I know the answer from your reaction," the doctor sighed. "You were with child, Sarah. But soon, he or she will pass from your womb."

Sarah touched her stomach reflexively as a new bout of tears overcame her. She had not even known about the life within her and yet, the sudden sense of loss was overwhelming.

"I cannot tell you how long, Sarah. However, I can tell you with certainty that whatever harm came to you, that is also what came to your unborn child. It could not be withstood." The doctor spoke slowly and the words exchanged between them made Sarah feel as though her head was in a cloud. His voice became muffled and she hardly noticed when Luke came into the room.

"Sarah? Are you okay?" he asked.

She looked up at Luke and shook her head. "Please, take me home." Luke took her by the hand and said goodbye to the doctor. They walked home in silence although Sarah knew that Luke wanted to know what had happened.

Sarah walked up the steps to her house and before she walked inside, Luke said to her, "I am not sure what has happened, but I hope you are okay. Remember, God has a plan for us all, but you do not have to be alone during this time."

At his words, Sarah turned around and Luke could see the sadness in her eyes. He did not want to press her for information she did not want to give him, but he was also unsure of what to say to her that might offer any sort of hope.

She sat down on the steps and after a few moments, Luke joined her. They sat together in silence for a while before Sarah finally spoke.

"I left my other community because my husband would have killed me if I had stayed," she said softly. She could feel Luke straighten beside her and she turned to look in his direction to judge his reaction. "Do you think this makes me a bad person?"

"Why do you believe that, Sarah? Why do you say he would have killed you?"

"Because," Sarah whispered, "he killed our son." Sarah went on to explain the incident where she and Jacob had been running through the field in the rain. She told Luke how when her husband had come home, he was so upset to find the house wet from the two of them. He pushed Sarah to the ground while she was clutching on to Jacob. He was barely two years old at that time. Her husband pulled her up by her hair and threw her against the well and she had hit her head so hard, she could hardly see straight. All she could see was that he was reaching for Jacob who was crying on the floor. All she could do was beg for his mercy, but he had none to give. He threw his son against the wall with such force that Sarah heard a sickening crack. She crawled over to where her son lay on the ground, but he did not move.

"I couldn't stay there," Sarah said between tears. "I have begged God for forgiveness and I truly believe he led me here so that I could start over."

"Sarah," Luke took her hand in his and pressed against his forehead. He looked up at her with such a fierce expression and said, "Sarah, you are safe here. We will not ever let anything hurt you. I will not ever let anything hurt you. Do you hear me?"

Sarah nodded her head and brushed the stray tears from her face.

"I think I will go lie down," she said softly. Luke watched her as she stood from her spot and walked inside, closing the door quietly behind her.

He had heard the doctor earlier—she had been with child and because of what that man had done, she had lost it. He had been the reason she lost two children. Luke could not bear the idea of someone harming Sarah and he struggled with this as he walked home and he wondered, not for the first time, why God had chosen such a difficult path for such a gracious woman.

As Luke walked inside of his house, both his sister and mother were waiting to question how his walk went, but after seeing his expression, they each retreated quietly to the kitchen. Luke went into his own bedroom and put his head against the pillow.

He reached for the bible which he kept by his bed and flipped open to a chapter in Romans. His eyes scanned the page and then landed on this passage, "Not only so, but we also glory in our sufferings, because we know that suffering produces perseverance; perseverance, character; and character, hope. And hope does not put us to shame, because God's love has been poured out into our hearts through the Holy Spirit, who has been given to us."

And suddenly Luke understood. Sarah had been chosen for such a path because she would be able to rise above it—rise above it and cast the light of her faith onto others, giving hope to those who had forgotten the word.

Chapter 4: Beginnings

The following morning Luke walked to Sarah's house before the sun had fully risen. He could not wait to tell her what had happened to him the previous night.

He walked up to her door and knocked softly. He waited patiently and right when he was going to knock again, Sarah opened the door. Her face was flushed, no doubt wondering who could be at her house at such an hour. Luke stole a moment to really appreciate her beauty—her chestnut brown hair peeking out from beneath her hastily placed bonnet and her hazel eyes which looked greener than brown in the early morning light.

"Luke, what are you doing here so early?"

"I had to come see you, Sarah. I was so vexed by your story yesterday, and I could not understand why it would happen to someone like you. I continued to think about what you had said to me earlier in the day—that you do not want to know information which the Lord does not share with you. And I was trying to follow the same thought process as you showed me, but I couldn't. So, I reached for my bible in search of the answer. And look! This is what he showed me." Luke handed her his bible and pointed to the passage which he had read the night before.

He watched Sarah as she read it and he could see her familiar light reigniting within her heart.

"Luke," Sarah said slowly. "I think that I was meant to meet you. I believe the Lord sent you into my life in my darkest hour to ensure that I would not lose faith."

Luke nodded and took Sarah's hand in his own. "And you," he said. "He sent you into my life so that you might restore the hope in my own heart." Sarah smiled at Luke and descended the steps. Together, they traced her favorite path along the river and she told Luke about the triumphant song of the river as it passed over the obstacles it was presented with.

Luke looked at Sarah and said, "Listen closer, Sarah. That is *your* song."

AMISH SECOND CHANCES

STEPHANIE SWIFT

Sarah stared longingly out the front window of the farmer's market and sighed. Only four days remained until Christmas and the sidewalk was packed with shoppers rushing to find last-minute gifts. Multi-colored lights glowed from the store windows across the street, and the snow was just starting to fall.

Any other time, the picturesque view would've made her excited for the holiday, but right now it was just giving her a massive headache. Unlike last year, she would be spending this Christmas alone, and that was enough to make her want to cancel the holiday altogether.

Sarah shuffled her feet against the tile floor as she made her way to the door so she could lock up. It had been a long day, and she was worn out – physically and emotionally. After listening to the happy chit-chat between her customers all day, she craved the peace and quiet of her apartment, where she could curl up on the sofa with a book and a steaming mug of coffee and not have to worry about the outside world... at least for a few hours.

Before she reached the door, however, it was suddenly flung open by two elderly women, Mary Martin and Ruth Coleman, whom she recognized from the Amish community on the outskirts of town where she'd once lived – before the divorce...before her life was turned completely upside down.

"Forgive me, Sarah!" Mary called. "I know you're getting ready to close, but I just need to buy a couple of things, and I promise I won't take long."

She wanted to push them back out onto the sidewalk, but they were rushing through the store before Sarah had the chance to object. She knew the Christian thing to do would be to bite her tongue and turn the other cheek, but it was difficult when these same two women were among the ones responsible for spreading rumors while she and her ex-husband, David, were going through their divorce proceedings.

Sarah went to the check-out counter to wait on them. She busied herself sorting through receipts and tidying up around the cash register, but she didn't miss the sideways glances the two women cast her way as they walked up and down the grocer aisles. They spoke to each other in soft whispers, and even though she couldn't make out the words, Sarah knew without a doubt she was the topic of conversation, which made her blood boil.

Nothing ever changed.

After what felt like an eternity, Mary and Ruth made their way to the register, and as Sarah rung up their items, she kept a smile glued to her face but avoided eye contact as much as possible.

It's almost over, Sarah. Just get them out the door and you can go home and relax. Be nice.

"We've missed seeing you in church the past few months," Ruth remarked. "How have you been?"

Sarah stood up a little straighter and squared her shoulders.

Here we go.

"I've been doing well. Just staying busy with work. How about you?"

They looked at each other again, and as Sarah put Mary's cash in the register and bagged her groceries, she caught the two of them exchanging smug smiles, which raised another red flag.

"Oh, we have no complaints," Ruth replied. "Sarah, I hope you don't mind me saying that we were all stunned when we learned David was still seeing that...that *woman*. I mean, the very nerve of him doing such a thing! I know you must be devastated."

It felt as if the wind had been thrust from Sarah's lungs as she leaned against the counter to keep from falling into a broken heap on the floor. David was still seeing Ann, the woman he was unfaithful with? No, that couldn't be true. He wouldn't do that.

Or would he? She thought he'd never cheat on her, but she'd been sorely mistaken about that too.

"Well, don't you worry, dear. We're on your side – always," Mary intervened, before giving what Sarah assumed was supposed to be a comforting pat on her hand. "*Denki* for letting us sneak in past closing time. I hope we see you at church this weekend for the special Christmas service."

She wanted to respond, but for some reason her mouth couldn't form words, so she nodded and smiled instead, which seemed to appease them. Mary picked up her groceries and the two of them headed for the entrance. When Sarah caught them snickering on their way out, she rushed to lock the door behind them before she received any more unwelcome visitors.

With the store finally empty, she flipped the business sign in the window to "closed" and turned off the lights. She could faintly hear Silent Night playing on the overhead speakers in the clothing store next door, and it was all a bit too much. Since the divorce, she'd basically existed on the hope that David was alone and regretting what he'd done to ruin their lives. Knowing he was happily existing with the woman he threw her away for was a kick in the gut...and heart.

Sarah leaned against the wall beside the window so she wouldn't be seen by the people walking past. The snow was falling faster now, and it wouldn't be long before everything was covered in a beautiful white blanket. Thoughts of her and David snuggling together on the front porch swing of their old home, watching the first snow of the season, flitted across her mind and made her eyes tear up. It was one of the traditions they'd looked forward to each year, but the first snowfall of this season had long come and gone, and she'd spent it alone, locked away inside her apartment.

Sarah pushed the thought from her mind and tried to imagine something happier. In a few short days she could take down the Christmas decorations. The holiday would be over with, and she could put it behind her and move on to a new year full of hope and possibilities.

It was small, but at least it was something to look forward too.

* * * *

David brought the truck to a stop in front of Palmer's Market and turned off the engine. The brick building loomed in front of him as he took a couple of deep breaths to calm his nerves. It was his first day making deliveries, but that wasn't what had him so anxious. It was also his first day back in the city.

When he took the part-time delivery job, he never expected to end up in the city limits of Lancaster – much less in the middle of Main Street. He was content to stay in the small town of Amory, twenty miles east of Lancaster, where he worked in construction full-time and kept to himself on his days off.

But being away from work gave him too much time to think about things that were better left alone, and so he took the part-time job.

Now he rarely had time to sit and think and that was a good thing – a very good thing.

David picked up a crate of milk jugs from the truck bed and walked to the front door entrance of the market, propping the crate on his hip momentarily so he could open the door. A bell chimed when he stepped inside, and he was immediately bombarded with several different aromas that assaulted his senses all at once, including bell peppers, celery, tomatoes, cinnamon and vanilla. The fragrances made his stomach growl from hunger, and he silently chided himself for leaving that morning without having breakfast first.

He spotted an employee helping a customer on the opposite side of the store, but her back was turned, so she didn't notice him walk in. David carried the crate of milk to the checkout counter and set it down. While he waited, he thumbed through a couple of magazines on a rack near the register, but it wasn't long before he heard footsteps approaching. He also heard what resembled a gasp, and when David looked up he was surprised to find his ex-wife, Sarah, staring back at him.

Over her clothing she wore a green apron with Palmer's Market stitched in bright yellow lettering across the front, and David groaned as he sent a quiet prayer to the heavens, asking the Lord to please open the floor and swallow him whole. If he'd known Sarah worked at one of his delivery stops, he never would've taken the job in the first place.

"David? What are you doing here?"

He didn't answer right away, and they stared at each other for the longest time, stopping only when the customer she'd been waiting on cleared her throat in a nonchalant way of letting her know she was ready to be checked out.

Sarah broke their gaze and went to the cash register, and David instinctively closed his eyes and inhaled the lavender scent of her shampoo as she walked by. At least, in a world where everything felt so uncertain, there was one thing he could rely on and that was Sarah and her obsession with lavender-scented beauty products.

She was just as beautiful as always, but she looked very different than the last time he'd seen her. The Amish attire he was used to seeing her in was replaced with a denim skirt and a purple floral-print blouse, and her hair wasn't hidden beneath a white bonnet anymore. Instead, it cascaded in soft auburn waves around her shoulders, and he could have sworn he saw a touch of make-up on her eyes and cheeks.

When the customer paid and left, there was an awkward silence between them, interrupted only by the tick-tock of the cuckoo clock on the wall behind the counter. He didn't know what to say or if he should try and start a conversation at all. Perhaps it would be best to just get the money for the milk and be on his way.

"You're making deliveries for Paul now?" she asked.

David followed her gaze to the crate and nodded. "He expanded his business, and he doesn't have time to make the deliveries himself, so I'm helping out a couple of days a week."

The conversation felt stilted and forced, but he didn't know how to change that. He was honestly surprised she chose to talk to him at all, especially since they hadn't parted on the best of terms.

"I'm sorry, Sarah. I know you said you never wanted to see me again after the divorce, but I honestly didn't know you worked here. If I did, I never would've taken the job."

He noticed the way she clenched her jaw, as if she didn't like his answer, but it was the truth. The last thing he wanted to do was make her angry or uncomfortable.

Sarah opened the register and removed some bills before slamming the drawer shut. When she thrust the money in his face, he took a cautious step backward to keep from being hit.

"Here," she said. "I'll let Mr. and Mrs. Palmer know they need to find another milk supplier. I'd hate for you to see me against your will."

David furrowed a brow as he took the money. "What is wrong with you? You're the one who said you never wanted to see me again. I was just trying to apologize."

Sarah leaned over the counter and he could see the fury blazing in her beautiful blue eyes. Even though the store was empty of customers, she kept her voice low, but there was no mistaking the way her voice trembled and seethed.

"You act like this is such a burden for you, but how do you think it makes me feel knowing you're still seeing Ann? Do you have any idea how humiliating that is for me?"

David's jaw slacked as he held up a hand to keep her from saying anything else. "Whoa...wait a second. What are you talking about? I'm not seeing Ann. I haven't seen or spoken to her since you and I went our separate ways."

She was speechless at first, but he detected something else in her gaze that made his heart thump a little faster. Relief, perhaps? He knew it couldn't be love, because he'd ruined that a long time ago.

"Mary Martin and Ruth Coleman told me you were still with her."

David's face flushed as the anger began to steep in his veins. He should have known those two busybodies were behind something like this.

"And you believed them?" he asked. "Sarah, you should know better than anyone else how much they love to gossip. They're two bitter old maids who have nothing better to do with their time than to try and make everyone around them miserable."

She nodded, but she didn't say anything, and the awkwardness returned. David put the money inside the zippered bank bag Paul gave him and made a move to leave. He'd heard enough, and he wasn't interested in wasting time arguing over nonsense.

"I have four more deliveries to make, so I should be going. I hope you have a Merry Christmas, Sarah."

David turned to leave, but Sarah reached out and grabbed his arm to stop him. The warmth from her touch seared through the fabric of his shirt and sent a shiver racing up his spine.

"I'm sorry, David. You're right. I should've given more thought to where the information was coming from and not jump to conclusions."

The soft lull of her voice pierced his heart, and for the millionth time, he wished he could take back the hurt he caused her – the hurt he inflicted on her and so many other people with his lapse in judgement.

"Are you happy, Sarah? I know you might find this hard to believe, but I truly want you to be happy. You deserve it more than anyone else I know."

He saw tears swell in the corners of her eyes, and he swallowed hard to keep from getting emotional.

"I am happy," she replied.

She looked away when she said it, and he could tell by the tone of her voice that she wasn't being completely honest, but he wasn't about to pry because he knew it was none of his business. For all he knew, she had moved on and was seeing someone else.

David inhaled deeply. The thought of her with another man made his insides twist into a painful knot, so he changed the subject to keep from dwelling on it. "If you'll show me where the freezer is, I'll put this milk away for you before I leave."

Sarah motioned for him to follow her and as he picked up the crate and tagged along behind her, he tried not to watch her every move. Still, it was hard not to notice the way her hair swished around her shoulders when she walked or the way the lights danced off her porcelain complexion. There were many things he missed about their relationship and being able to run his fingertips over her soft skin was high on the list.

"Are you spending Christmas with your family?" she asked.

David opened the freezer and organized the milk on the metal rack by shuffling the older bottles to the front and placing the newer bottles behind them.

"They're spending Christmas with my sister and her family in Ohio. I was invited, but you know how much I hate flying."

She smiled at his comment, and he breathed a small sigh of relief, hoping they were finally past the unease from their earlier conversation. "What about you? Is your family staying at the house this Christmas?"

And just like that, her smile was gone.

"I don't live there anymore," she replied. "I've been renting the apartment upstairs from the Palmer's for about eight months now, and it's too small for guests."

David was stunned. He'd never imagined Sarah not living in the home they built when they were newlyweds. It had always been such a huge part of her life, and she'd spent so much time decorating and taking care of it.

"I don't understand. Did you sell the house?"

Sarah closed the freezer door and began making her way back to the checkout counter, leaving David no other choice but to follow.

"I still have the house, but I couldn't live there anymore. It was too painful," she admitted. "Plus, I was tired of living around such nosey neighbors and being the talk of the town, so I moved here to get away from it all."

He felt another kick to his gut, and he didn't know how to respond. For as long as he lived he would never get over the guilt of kissing Ann and losing Sarah's trust. Add to that the guilt he now felt over Sarah leaving their community to get away from the heartache and it was almost too much to bear. He had been shunned and she couldn't live there in peace. Oh, what he wouldn't give if he could start over and make things right.

"I'm so sorry, Sarah. I didn't know."

A customer walked in before she had the chance to reply, and David took that as his cue to leave. He was so downtrodden and his spirits were so low he could have easily crawled out on his hands and knees.

"I hope you have a Merry Christmas, David. I mean that."

He gave her a half-hearted smile and returned the sentiment before turning to go, and as he closed the door behind him, he peered one last time through the window and watched as she waited on her customer. Would there ever come a day when the guilt wouldn't feel as if it were crushing him?

Somehow, he doubted it.

* * * *

Sarah watched from her second-floor bedroom window as a marching band from one of the local high schools passed by on the street below. It was Christmas Eve and the annual Lancaster Christmas parade was well under way. They were already thirty minutes into the parade and she could still see a lengthy line of floats and bands extending along the length of Main Street and beyond.

Sarah grinned as she watched the children lining the sidewalk across the street jump up and down excitedly when the float carrying Old Saint Nick passed by. He threw candy into the crowd and the kids scattered, trying to grab as much as they could fit into their pockets before someone else snatched it up. It made her laugh seeing how determined they were.

Although the temperature had dropped considerably over the past couple of days, the frigid air didn't appear to dampen anyone's spirits. She was grateful the Palmer's had given her three days off work to enjoy the holiday, but she wished there was more to do besides watching the parade from her lone spot by the window. She could've joined the others on the sidewalk, but it seemed pointless watching the parade by herself while everyone around her enjoyed it with their loved ones.

Sarah blew her warm breath against the cold window and traced a heart in the fog on the glass as her thoughts turned to David. He'd looked so handsome when he visited the store. She was used to seeing him in Amish clothing, but she had to admit that the jeans, company work shirt, and boots made him look more rugged and masculine. His black hair was cut short and he even had a bit of stubble on his face. Since their divorce, she'd often pondered whether he'd settled into a different Amish village somewhere else, but seeing the way he was dressed answered that question.

She couldn't help but wonder if he'd found someone to spend the holiday with since he wasn't able to visit his family. He seemed surprised when she mentioned living in the apartment, and she frowned when she considered the possibility that she might have to sell the house someday. She had no plans to return, and since David had been shunned, there really was no point in keeping it. Letting go of it, however, was something else entirely.

They'd put their heart and soul into building the small wood frame house – right down to the extra bedroom they hoped to convert to a nursery someday. But then Ann entered their lives and everything changed in an instant. She could still recall the night David confessed of their interlude as if it were yesterday, and the pain was still just as raw.

Sarah rested her head against the window pane and thought for a moment. Could she really call it an interlude? They'd shared one kiss that David swore on many occasions was initiated by Ann. She feverishly shook her head. No, a sin was still a sin in God's eyes, whether it was just one kiss or one night of passion, and that one kiss had broken their sacred marriage bond.

A knock on her door startled her from her reverie, and as Sarah went to answer it, she forced the troubling thoughts from her mind. It was Christmas, after all – a joyous holiday meant to celebrate the Savior's birth, and it shouldn't be spent dwelling on parts of her past she couldn't change.

When Sarah opened the door, she found Mrs. Palmer standing on the other side. The elderly woman was dressed in seasonal clothing, from the jingle bells tied to her shoelaces straight to the toy reindeer antlers on her head. The front of her work apron was decorated with a multitude of Christmas buttons and pins, and she caught a glimpse of Grandma Elf stitched across the front of her red and green sweater. She had to admit she looked adorable.

Sarah's grandparents passed away when she was a child, but if she had the chance to choose another one to call her own, Mrs. Palmer would be at the top of the list.

"Good morning, Sarah! Merry Christmas Eve!"

It was rare to see the elderly woman without a smile on her face, and as she wrapped Sarah in a warm hug, she smiled when she detected the faint scent of sugar cookies. It was also rare not to smell some type of savory goodness on her clothes or in her salt-and-pepper hair, since Mrs. Palmer loved to bake and did it often.

"These are for you. Fresh from the oven."

She handed Sarah a small metal tin, and her mouth watered when she lifted the lid and found an assortment of cookies inside. Chocolate chip, oatmeal, peanut butter – and just as she suspected...sugar cookies.

"Thank you so much, Mrs. Palmer. They smell divine."

The smile on her cherub face was enough to melt Sarah's heart, and she felt like kicking herself because she had nothing to give her in return. Having grown up in an Amish household her whole life, she rarely received gifts or material things for the holidays, so this new way of celebrating was something she was still trying to get used to.

"Oh! This is for you too, dear. Someone named David called the store a little while ago looking for you, and I told him you weren't working. I wasn't sure if you wanted him to know your cell phone number or not, so I asked for his number instead."

Sarah almost dropped the cookie tin as she took the piece of paper from Mrs. Palmer's hand with shaky fingers.

"I better get downstairs. We'll be closing early and heading to my granddaughter's house to spend Christmas with her and her family. I'll see you Monday morning."

Sarah hugged her one more time. "Thank you again, Mrs. Palmer. I hope you and your family have a wonderful Christmas."

Mrs. Palmer gave her an affectionate squeeze. "You too, dear."

When they said their goodbyes and Sarah closed the door, she leaned against it for several long minutes, staring at the paper in her hand with David's phone number scribbled on it. The ten digits beckoned like a light in the dark, but she couldn't help but feel a little hesitant.

What could he possibly want?

More than a little intrigued, Sarah went back to her bedroom and retrieved her cell phone from the nightstand beside her bed and punched in the numbers. Her heart beat so rapidly she thought it might pound right out of her chest, and she took a couple of deep breaths to try and remain calm. After two rings, she heard a familiar deep voice on the other end of the line.

"Hello?"

Sarah sat down on the edge of her bed before her wobbly knees landed her on the floor.

"Hey David. It's Sarah. I was just returning your phone call. Is everything alright?"

There was a long pause before he answered, and Sarah worried she may have started the conversation off on the wrong foot. She wasn't used to talking on the phone, and she couldn't even remember the last time she'd received a call from a man other than her father or Mr. Palmer.

"Would you be angry with me if I told you I want us to spend Christmas together?" he asked.

Although spending the holiday with her ex-husband should've been the last thing on her mind, she had to confess she felt a little excited over the idea. Thanksgiving had come and gone with nothing to show for it besides leftover turkey from her dinner with the Palmer's and she'd been dreading Christmas ever since.

"If you don't want to, I totally understand," he continued.

Sarah went to her bedroom window and watched the paradegoers having a good time on the sidewalk below. If she said no, what else did she have to look forward to besides watching the rest of the parade? It would be ending soon and then what was there to do – spend the rest of the holiday weekend doing crossword puzzles or watching television?

"Sarah? Are you still there?"

She turned away from the window and focused her attention on David. "What did you have in mind?"

There was another short pause as Sarah waited anxiously for his answer.

"I would like to cook for you," he replied. "Would it bother you if I buy the ingredients and come over to your apartment to fix dinner for you? If that makes you uncomfortable, we could always have dinner at my house."

Her mind drifted back to the many meals they'd cooked together while they were married and she smiled. She did her best, but she couldn't deny the fact that he was by far a better chef than she could ever hope to be.

"I wouldn't mind if you cooked here."

For some reason, just saying it made her feel giddy inside.

"Great! Can I come over around 5:00 and get started or is that too early?" he asked.

She didn't have to see his face to know he was grinning because she could detect it in his voice.

"Five o'clock is fine. There's an enclosed stairway beside the market that leads to the second floor. When you get here, press the buzzer by the door, and I'll let you in."

They talked a little while longer before hanging up and Sarah remained where she was, mulling over their conversation in her mind. She hoped she hadn't made a huge mistake, but there was only one way to find out.

* * * *

David juggled the grocery bags around in his arms so he could press the buzzer, and he finally managed after a couple of unsuccessful attempts. When Sarah appeared, and opened the door for him, he tried not to laugh as the two of them haphazardly climbed the stairway like two circus clowns trying to stay upright on a unicycle.

"Good heavens!" she exclaimed. "Did you buy the whole store?"

David laughed. "I know...I know. I kind of went overboard."

When they made their way inside her apartment, he followed her to the kitchen and set the bags on top of the counter.

"I get the feeling you're trying to impress me," she said with a wink.

David chucked as he started unloading the bags. "Maybe I am."

As she took the grocery items and placed them in the cabinets and refrigerator, he tried not to ogle her, but she looked so beautiful. The red dress she wore showed off her curves and her hair was tied loosely at the base of her neck with a festive ribbon. She had on lip gloss, and it took every ounce of strength he had not to pull her close and kiss her. He didn't want to assume she'd gotten dressed up just for him, but he did feel a little bit hopeful.

"I know this probably isn't what you'd call a traditional Christmas meal, but I remember how much you love spaghetti," he commented.

Sarah smiled as she retrieved some pots and pans for cooking. "It's always a good time for spaghetti – holiday or no holiday."

When David started preparing the meal, he was pleasantly surprised when Sarah joined in to help instead of leaving him to do it all alone. It felt like old times being in the kitchen with her, and although he worried at first there may be some awkwardness between them, he was happy when that proved not to be the case. They cooked the meal in silence, but it was a comfortable silence, interrupted only by the soft strains of Christmas music streaming from a radio in Sarah's living room.

David took the pot of spaghetti noodles and drained the water in the kitchen sink while Sarah retrieved the garlic toast from the oven, and as they brought their dinner to the table, he thought back to the many nights they'd dined at the kitchen table in their home. He wanted to mention it, but he also didn't want to risk ruining the moment, so he kept his thoughts to himself.

Baby steps, David...baby steps.

David pulled a chair out for Sarah, and when she sat down, he didn't miss the way her cheeks flushed, which he hoped was a sign she was enjoying his company. He took a chance and sat down in the chair beside her, instead of across the table from her, and he was relieved when she didn't object. They both bowed their heads and closed their eyes, and as David said grace over the meal, his heart fluttered wildly when Sarah reached out and held his hand, like she used to do when they were married. Perhaps it was just something she was accustomed to doing, but he took it as a positive step in the right direction.

They talked about the usual things over dinner, like the weather and work, and although David wanted desperately to talk about something more personal, he was determined to wait for the right moment.

"Do you mind me asking if you still attend church regularly?" she inquired. "I noticed you don't wear Amish clothing anymore, so I was curious."

David sat up a little straighter in his seat while contemplating his answer. Could this be the right moment he was waiting for? It felt as if God was opening a door, and he took a deep breath, not wanting to mess up what might be his only opportunity to tell Sarah how he felt. He cleared his throat before attempting to speak.

"My boss invited me to visit his church a few months ago, and I attend services every Sunday. When I was shunned from the village, I was afraid I might lose my way, but my faith in God is even stronger now. I finally realized I don't have to be a member of a certain church to know He loves me and that I'm forgiven."

David held his breath as he waited for her to reply. He hoped he didn't come across as harsh, but it was the truth. When Bishop Tucker and the elders in the village decided to shun him instead of accepting his apology for his indiscretion, he thought his life might never be the same, but he prayed for and received God's forgiveness, and that was all that mattered.

Sarah put down her fork and napkin and leaned back in her chair. She laced her fingers together on top of her lap, and she was quiet for a long time, but when she looked at him, he was relieved to see her smiling.

"I'm glad to hear you say that. After our divorce, I saw a side to the community I didn't like, and that's why I decided to move. I still went to their services every week, but it was never the same, and I eventually stopped going. A couple of women who work at the clothing store next door invited me to their church, and I've been going there ever since."

Her whole face lit up while she talked about it, and it was easy to see what a positive influence it had on her life. It felt as if a weight had been lifted from his shoulders after worrying for so long that his wrongdoing may have affected her spiritual life too, but it was plainly evident her faith was still as strong as ever.

David took a chance and reached out to hold her hand.

"Sarah, do you think there will ever come a day when you will be able to forgive me?"

He half expected her to say "no", but when she smiled at him, he felt a small glimmer of hope.

"I forgave you a long time ago, David. Forgetting what happened hasn't been as easy to accomplish, but I'm working on that."

He sighed.

"So, I'm guessing a reconciliation might be too much to wish for?" he asked.

Sarah placed her free hand on top of his arm and gently caressed his skin, making his heart leap into his throat. Her touch was soft and sent a warm current rushing through his whole body. He was so worried the moment might pass he didn't dare move a muscle.

"I wouldn't say it's completely out of the question," she replied with a grin.

They remained that way for the longest while, simply enjoying each other's company, and when they resumed eating, the conversation flowed freely. His heart soared every time she laughed, and when they began reminiscing about special moments from their past, the ray of hope he clung to seemed to burn a little brighter.

After dinner, as Sarah cleared the table and David cleaned the kitchen, they accidentally bumped into each other, and when he wrapped his arms around her waist to keep her from falling, he was ecstatic when she didn't try to push him away. He probably shouldn't have held on as long as he did, but it felt so good having her in his arms again, and he wanted the moment to last for as long as possible.

"I don't think there will ever come a day when holding you like this doesn't feel perfect and right," he whispered.

She looked up at him, and his heart pounded when he saw the desire in her soulful blue eyes.

"David...do you think it would be possible for us to start over?" she asked. "I don't want to rush this though. If we do try again, I would like to take it slowly."

David traced her jawline with his fingertips, loving the way her body still trembled at his touch. "I believe we can do whatever we set our minds to. I know I hurt you, Sarah, and I'm so sorry, but I promise I will never hurt you again. I hope you know that."

When she stood on her tip-toes and tenderly kissed his lips, David knew he received his answer...and the second chance he longed for.

AN INJURED AMISH HEART

ALICE EVANS

<u>Prologue</u>

Love is more than a feeling. And it isn't something so simplistic as an idea... It is this positive, electric energy that flows throughout your entire body and radiates outward. No matter who you are or what you have experienced, everyone is capable of experiencing this phenomenon. One of the greatest aspects of being human is our capacity to love; but there isn't just one kind of love, there are several facets of love. As I theorize, love isn't something so simple as one idea or definition. Whether it is familial love for those closest to you, or a love so strong it feels like your heart is going to rip right out of your chest for the one person God has designed for you; love is the most powerful source we can ever hope to know.

Unfortunately, there is a flaw in this innocent desire to love. If you ask someone to tell you why they were with someone, the typical response is because their heart told them to and they couldn't think of anything or anyone else. Cheesiness aside, this brings up an issue. Can we trust our heart to make the right choice?

"How do you know when you meet this person that they are the one for you? How can you differentiate the one, perfect person from the sea of hundreds or even thousands? There is no guarantee that the person you meet is the perfect person for you. You may not end up with someone perfect, but you may end up with someone who is perfect for you.

But then again....

What happens when you end up with the wrong person? Whether by proximity or a series of misleading circumstances, and then one or both parties are injured. Keeping your heart in check is one of the hardest struggles a human can face. Because we can't help who we love, and there is no guarantee who our heart picks is someone whose heart will also pick us. Such a thing happened to Lovina Smith. Rain fell upon her window pane, as she continued to suppress her tears. Her mind raced as her final conversation with him flashed before her eyes:

"I'm so glad you were able to come over to see me Luke. It feels like I haven't heard from you in ages. Don't you think that as your betrothed I should get to see you more often?"

"We need to talk, Lovina."

"Oh, I know. We have to start planning; well we really just need to decide where we will be living after we are married. My parents left me this house, which is good sized; but if we want to have kids someday-"

"Lovina!" Lovina was shocked by this sudden change of tone. In the four years they had known each other he had never raised his voice to her.

"L-Luke... what's wrong?"

"I... we... I don't think we fit together like we used to."

"Luke, what are you saying? Do you... do you not want to marry me anymore?"

"Look. I get this probably is the farthest thing from what you expected, but I need to do what is right for me, and frankly this," Luke gestured between himself and Lovina, *"isn't doing it for me anymore."*

"What do you mean you don't want to get married anymore? Is it something I did? What's going on with you?"

"Exactly what I said. Why are you being so thick about this?" Luke strode towards the door, about to fling it open.

"Well can you at least explain to me why you are doing this? You owe me that much Luke!"

"You know exactly why." Lovina's heart fell out of her chest and onto the floor. As Luke strode back towards her, she could almost feel his footsteps stomp all over the love she had gifted him for so long.

"That's it? What did you find someone else willing to satisfy you?"

"Yes."

Lovina slapped her hands against her window, forcing the memories to stop. The tears, now spilling out of her eyes, caused her to wonder whether it was still raining, or if her vision was just blurring. All the pain she felt, all of love she gave him for four years, all washed away.

"God, please give me the strength.... The strength to overcome."

<u>Chapter One</u>

After that day it became almost impossible for Lovina to notice the passage of time. Days, months, weeks, or even years; she wouldn't have been able to tell. Though days continued to pass, in her mind, she was still stood, frozen, in that room. That plain, simple room that once made her beam with joy. The slatted blonde wood beams and the oaky smell in the air, now forever taint the memories she held so dear. Lovina would stare around the room to see the memory of her father whittling as her mother prepared for supper and she'd once feel a surge of relief. Now...

Now, she can't think about the good times in her home without remembering Luke. From the moment he stepped into her life, that room became the setting. Even in the first moment they met, Luke stepped over the threshold and into her heart. At the time, Luke was her father's apprentice and had taken over her father's business when he passed away three years ago to a bout of pneumonia.

Lovina only ever had one job in her life: working at her godmother's bakery. "Fisher's Bakery" had been in the family for generations. It wasn't a stately building; some may even refer to it as a shack, to which Lovina would quickly defend. To her, it wasn't just a slightly run-down building... to her it was where all the brightest memories of her childhood were made.

Lovina's earliest memories surround her godmother from when she was a little girl; running in after her mother to find her godmother - Cynthia Fisher - covered in white powder and with fallen strands of auburn hair plastered against her forehead. She has no children of her own, so Cynthia's plan had always been to pass the business on to Lovina. Loving her more than her own family, Cynthia watched on as her beloved godchild worked mindlessly behind the counter. Trying to figure out what to do, Cynthia invited two of Lovina's closest friends to discuss options.

"There must be something we haven't tried yet... I mean, she's just... It's like she's not even there anymore."

"I know... she's only been to the store and home for six months. This isn't healthy," Sara Dixon responded. Sara's eyes plead with her friend's frame as she looked on in pity.

"But what can we do? She doesn't want to talk about anything, and she refuses to admit that she needs help," a silken voice replied. Teresa Miller - an old school friend of Lovina's - had come at Cynthia's bequest. She recently had been married and moved to a town a few counties over. However, as soon as she got word that it was Lovina who was in trouble, she had no issue dropping everything and returning home.

"You guys know I can hear you right?" A bent over Lovina said from behind the bakery counter. The women quickly hold their tongues, unaware of how loud their counsel had been.

"Well then maybe, you should try to listen to what we are saying."

"Yes Lovina. I mean, how do you expect to-" Lovina was sure that they were still telling her how to get over how distraught and disgusted she felt, but she couldn't bear to listen to them anymore. Blocking them out, she moved back to the ovens and continued to bake alone with her thoughts.

As Lovina walked home from the bakery that night, it was hard for her not to feel the weight of her closest confidants fall on her heart. A haze still lingered over her thoughts, but Lovina was beginning to feel that something has to change. The ringing of thunder in her ears shook her from her confusion. Her eyes flash to the sky right as the clouds open up and the floodgates break. She can hear her mother's words in her ears,

"Don't run in the rain, you will only get wetter." But her reaction was unchanged. She took off through the streets that were quickly turning to mud. Her feet began to struggle to force herself through. As she takes one more larger step, Lovina falls, headfirst into the street. Feeling an almost cosmic sense of irony, Lovina can't find the will to pull herself up out of the mud.

After lying there for more time than she would care to admit to, she raised her head to see a pair of boots striding towards her. Quickly looking upon herself to adjust to prevent any scrutiny, by the time she turned her eyes back to the sky, her gaze was met with a firm hand.

"Are you alright, miss?" Lovina was at a loss for words as she gazed into his eyes. Lovina never really paid much attention to appearances, but with the man in front of her now, it was impossible to ignore. From his sharp jawline to his piercing silver eyes, Lovina had never met a man so handsome. He offers his hand once more, shaking Lovina from her state, and she takes it as he lifts her to her feet.

"Thank you, sir."

"What's a lady like you doing out here alone with no umbrella? This isn't exactly the best weather for a casual stroll." Lovina laughs as the man holds his jacket over her head.

"I was on my way home from the bakery where I work and I thought I could make it home before the rain, but I guess luck was not in my favor today." The man looked over her muddy appearance and stifled a laugh.

"Well, I am on my way home as well, is there somewhere I can take you on the way?"

"Oh no, thank you, but you don't have to do that."

"Miss, I wouldn't feel right about leaving you on your own. I mean, what would happen if you fell in the mud again?" Lovina met the man's eyes again; but this time they were sparkling.

"Well, I am headed down this road a bit further, where is your home?"

"I live down the same way. I am staying with Deacon Macon and his wife until I can finish my home."

"Alright, well if we are already heading in the same direction, I guess it would be alright for you to escort me home." The man smiled and held out his arm, which she took and they continued down the road. Though they didn't say much outside of the normal pleasantries - who they were, where they are from, and what they do - Lovina couldn't remember a time when she had felt this relaxed as she walked home. By the time they arrived at her door, it felt as if no time had passed at all.

"Thank you for escorting me. I really do appreciate the gesture. I wish I could repay you for sparing me a bit of my dignity."

"Think nothing of it. I just did what any man should do."

"Well I would still like to show my gratitude in some way... How about you come by the bakery tomorrow and you can walk me home and I can bring you some food?"

"That sounds like something I would be interested in."

"Good. I will see you tomorrow night then, Mr... I'm so sorry it seems I never got your name."

"Thomas. Thomas Elton. And you are?"

"Lovina."

"Well Miss Lovina, I will see you tomorrow night." And with the tip of his hat, he backed off of her porch, and continued down the path.

Lovina had to remind herself to breathe as she gazed at his figure disappear around the corner at the end of the lane. As she closed her door, her back thudded against it - cementing her disbelief in what she has just done. Inviting a man - not just to visit her place of work, but to walk her home for a second time. As much as she had managed to shock herself, she had to turn that emotion off in order to get herself ready for the day that was to come. She quickly cleaned herself off and hung the wet clothes out to dry before wrapping herself in a blanket and falling quickly asleep in anticipation of the day that was to come.

<u>Chapter Two</u>

"Lovina what are you waiting for? You have been pinning out that window all day." Cynthia couldn't understand this overnight shift in behavior. Lovina's behavior was also a shock to the ladies at the bakery. Her hair wasn't slicked back in a bun, but her auburn locks flowed over her shoulders and her face was brighter than they had seen it in months.

"What do you mean?" Lovina asked without so much as batting her eyes as her gaze continued out the window. The ladies shared looks and whispered to one another trying to pinpoint what has caused the flippant change in their friend when all of a sudden the door opened.

"I am sorry, but we are about to close-" Cynthia bit her tongue before she could finish dismissing the man now standing in the entrance. Lovina's eyes met his immediately, giving her a better look in the daylight than she got the night before. His silver eyes sparkled the same, if not more intensely with the help of the sun's rays; and his strong figure wasn't menacing, but warm and open. She also was able to get a better look at his strong jaw and ruffled copper hair and stubble that adorned his face.

"I'm sorry for my lateness."

"Oh no, you are right on time. I was just about to leave." As much as the other women wanted to take in every second of this exchange, they knew that it was not right to spy. Quickly Cynthia pushed the ladies towards the back door and excused herself in an attempt of being discreet, but in her stuttering of words and lack of ability to keep her eyes from darting from the pair, discretion was not something that she was able to achieve.

"I apologize for my aunt. She can be a bit much sometimes."

"I don't mind. She reminds me a lot of my grandmother, God rest her soul." The pair exchange a smile and Lovina grabs a box from behind the counter.

"Here you are, as I promised."

"You know, you really didn't have to go to the trouble."

"I wanted to. This is one of the few things that I seem to be good at, so let me use my skill to thank you." Thomas smiled as Lovina handed over the box. He then offered his arm and escorted her out of the building and down the lane.

Before the pair realized, this became a regular thing. Everyday at closing time, Thomas would enter the bakery - sometimes a bit dirtier than other times depending upon what his work was that day - and Lovina would be waiting for him to walk her home. This went on for almost four months before Thomas decided to be brave.

"So, I am having dinner with Deacon Macon and his wife this evening for the first time in my house."

"You finished the house? That's so exciting."

"Yes... well I was wondering if maybe you would like to join us tonight for dinner." Lovina was ecstatic to hear this question as it floated through the air. "I mean, if you already have plans don't worry about it or anything-"

"I would love to come." Thomas let a big smile spread across his face.

"Great! Dinner will be around 7. Do you want me to come and fetch you or...?"

"I can call upon the Deacon. I am sure we can all walk over together. Besides, it has been so long since I've spoken with Mrs. Macon." Thomas nodded is head in understanding, as the air now buzzed with their intertwined excitement for the evening to come.

Lovina put on her newest and cleanest dress and fixed her hair up all pretty before walking a few houses down to meet the Macons. As she walked up their path, Mrs. Macon opened the door and greeted Lovina with a warm hug.

"Lovina, dear, it's been too long."

"I agree. I am sorry I haven't been by to visit all that much."

"My dear, you never have to apologize to me for anything. You're parents did right by me, and I know that they would have approved of the decision you made, despite how difficult it was for you." Lovina's smile dropped for a moment, but Mrs. Macon felt the need to quickly amend her statement.

"What I mean to say- I mean- Under the same circumstances, I would never have been able to- to-"

"Mrs. Macon, I thought we agreed not to bring up any of those unhappy moments tonight. Especially with all of the happiness that may enter our lives after tonight." Deacon took his wife's hands and made her beautiful smile spread across her face. Deacon turns his head to Lovina, his well groomed facade couldn't hide his excitement and his overwhelming emotions for something she didn't quite understand.

"Deacon, thank you for escorting me this evening along with your wife. I know when we are together we can be a bit much."

"It is no problem at all Lovina. I know that this dinner is something Thomas has been wanting to plan since he met you. I don't know what you have done, but in the whole time I have known him, he has never been as positive or as happy as he has been since he's been courting you."

"Did he say that, did he use those words?"

"Which words?"

"Daniel Macon, do not tease the poor girl." Lovina bore holes into the older couple. Praying that the words she heard meant what she thought they meant. Deacon looked onto Lovina as his eyes answered her question without him needing to utter even one syllable. Lovina's face flushes, unable to keep her happiness from revealing itself. The Macons looked on Lovina with such love and care as they ushered her out of their home onto the street and - in their minds - into the rest of her life.

Thomas had been stressing all day. Was his house clean enough for her? Was the food he prepared good enough for her? All of these questions and more flooded through his mind until the knock came at his door. Fear ratcheting up with every step he took towards the door, he turned the knob, and then suddenly it was like everything had melted away. The instant he saw Lovina's face, all of the fears, doubts, and confusion melted away and he was blissfully happy.

The Macons felt the connection between the young couple the moment the door opened; and they couldn't have been happier. After having Thomas live with them for all those months while his house was being built, and after knowing Lovina practically her entire life, they couldn't imagine a better scenario for either of them. Deacon did - however - clear his throat after an uncomfortable amount of silence had passed.

The dinner went smoothly - much to Thomas's glee - and after some good conversation and a stroll around Thomas's property, the Macons decided to call it a night; however, Lovina decided to stay behind.

"Thank you for dinner."

"It was my pleasure, Lovina. But frankly, I feel that I owe you much more than one simple meal."

"You don't owe me anything, why do you keep saying that?"

"Because it's the truth." Lovina looked up at the man as he shuffled his feet. He seemed off somehow to her. His frame - usually so strong and firm - seemed more open and weaker in a sense. This change confused her, and she tried to meet his gaze in order to find out why his demeanor was so changed.

"Is everything alright? Did I do something wrong?"

"No! No, not at all!"

"Well then why won't you look at me? Everything was fine during dinner, but now it's like you can't even bring yourself to look at me..."

"I'm just..."

"Just what?"

"I'm afraid." Lovina nodded her head for him to explain further as to why he was so fearful. "I'm afraid of something I have been feeling and I am unsure as to how to proceed because I do not know how to discuss it with you without potentially ruining our friendship." Lovina moved across the room to him, gliding with each step, and placed her hands in his.

"Ask me. Please." Her eyes pleading for the question she had been waiting so long to receive from him. Thomas's eyes ignite as he holds her hands in his, but before he can get one word out, there is a knock at the door. Assuming that it is the Macons, Thomas yells towards the door,

"What did you forget Deacon?" A few moments of silence before the reply and then a voice spoke up that none of them expected:

"Lovina, we need to talk."

<u>Chapter Three</u>

Lovina was frozen. Inches from Thomas's warm embrace, the man who destroyed her world entered her gaze. She didn't know whether to laugh or cry; push Thomas away or hold him closer. Lovina's head lowered as she attempted to reign her thoughts in.

"Lovina, we need to talk?" She spat his words back at him as she turned to face him.

"I don't think you two have anything to discuss frankly." Thomas stated as he put himself between Luke and Lovina. He stood strong - however, Lovina could feel his muscles tense and hear his heartbeat quicken - as he stood as a protective barrier. Luke's gaze tore momentarily from Lovina to square off against the man in his way. He scoffed,

"And who are you to make her decisions for her?" Thomas looked upon Lovina, unsure of how to categorize their relationship to her former suitor. Lovina couldn't help but notice the stark contrasts between

"Luke, please. Now is not a good time."

"Oh! Now isn't a good time? And I suppose earlier at the diner was also a bad time?"

"Luke, I-"

"Wait, why didn't you tell me he showed up at the diner?" Thomas his voice tinged with concern, not the anger Lovina had expected. Before she could explain why she didn't tell him about her and Luke's earlier encounter, Luke decided it was a brilliant time to speak once more.

"You need to make your mind up Lovina. You can't love me but go run off anytime I'm not around."

"Run around?" Luke realized that it was too late to remove the foot from his mouth. "I never ran around on you." Lovina pushed down on Thomas's arms that were shielding her from the man who broke her spirit. "You left me for someone else simply because I wouldn't sleep with you until we were married. You threw away a four year courtship or relationship, whatever you want to call it; over pursuing the pleasures of the flesh."

"Lovina, it's not that simple."

"Of course it's that simple! When you left me, after all of my pleading and hoping and begging for you to reconsider, the only thing you told me as to why you were leaving is that I wouldn't sleep with you." Thomas's face fell as he saw the tears flowing angrily from the woman he had come to love. He makes a move to her, but Lovina's eyes flash towards him to stay exactly where he is.

"Lovina, please. Can we not have this conversation in front of-"

"I want him to hear. I need someone else to understand that I am not crazy for being as broken as I was."

"Wait... you never-"

"No. As angry as you made me and as broken as you left me, I never once shared with anyone that you left me for someone who would sleep with you."

"Why did you do that?"

"You were the golden boy of town. What would have happened if I slandered your name? I would have lost my credibility and I would be scorned for the town only loved me because they loved you." Luke's mind was swimming. At the time, he was convinced he was making the right decision, but now as he stood in front of the woman he left behind, and his once confident thoughts began to waiver. Thomas sees Luke's hesitation and takes what he believes to be his last chance. Moving once more into Lovina's bubble, he pushes the hair out of her face and tilts her chin to meet his gaze.

"Just say the word. Whatever you want from me, I'm here." His strong hands rest on her cheeks. Placing her hands on top of his, Lovina stroked his long fingers and saw herself in the reflection of his mirror like eyes. The image she saw shocked her. After months of being told that she had become gaunt and pale in coloring, the woman she saw in his eyes was strong and healthy.

"So that's how you see me."

"You are so much more to me than your shell. You always have been." Lovina's vision became blurry - as for the first time in she couldn't remember how long - she was crying for a reason other than sadness. Her hands, unbeknownst to her, rested on his chest before she circled them around his neck as she drew herself into him. As she sniffled into his shirt, Lovina began to take in every aspect of this moment. From the musty smell of wood from the shop to his strong arms holding her against him, making her feel that he would become her new foundation. As a smile spreads across her face, Lovina hears Luke clear his throat.

"Excuse me, but I would prefer if you removed your hands from my girl."

"What, so because she once agreed to marry you she was supposed to just sit around here pinning after you despite the fact that you skipped town for someone outside our way of life?" Luke's eyes flash to Lovina.

"How dare you tell a stranger about my personal business! I thought you were different!"

"ME?" Lovina's blood boiled in her veins as Luke tossed his accusations around the room. "You destroyed my life. You made a commitment to me, my parents - God rest their souls - and then just because you weren't happy with my opinions on the sanctity of marriage, you left."

"Well all of that is behind us now, we can move on together and grow back together. I never loved her like I love you; not even close."

"Then why did you leave me?" Lovina took four strong steps towards the man making her blood boil and her eyes overflow. "If you claim to love me so much, how could you have barred to leave me? Even if you couldn't overcome your sinful desires - or your human instincts as you will argue they were - why didn't you come back after you had been satisfied and begged my forgiveness?"

"Come on darling-"

"You don't get to call me that. You will address me properly if you wish to address me at all."

"Why are you being so stubborn? Women would kill for a man like me to offer you what I'm offering."

"What exactly are you offering her?" Thomas decided to re enter the drama unfolding in her living space. Luke's face hardened as his eyes shifted from Lovina to Thomas.

"I'm offering her a life; and a good one at that. I am a successful businessman and have plenty of money to where she can quit that stupid bakery job and come stay at home so we can start raising a family. Lovina has always wanted a family and I am prepared to provide her with that."

"I may want a family; but you of all people should know that bakery means everything to me." Lovina shocked both herself and the two men stood across from her with her outburst.

"Lovina-"

"I'm alright, Thomas." Lovina shares a sweet smile with Thomas before returning her gaze to Luke. "Let me make this as crystal clear as I possibly can: yes, I did once love you; but now you have made it impossible for me to ever forgive you. I may not have been able to see then because I was blinded by love, but you never actually learned anything about me. You don't know about why I love the bakery so much, and you will never understand why I can't forgive you for why you left."

"Are you sure this is the choice you want to make? You are choosing a hired hand over a business owner. You will never be wealthy."

"I don't need to be wealthy. After all of this time, I finally understand what it is that I have been looking so long for: I need to and I deserve to be happy." Turning to Thomas, her eyes shed their last tear. "And Thomas makes me irrevocably happy." Thomas strides over to her as her words hit his ears. He threw his arms around her waist and hoists her up and spins her around. The loving pair embraced as Luke, ashamed and embarrassed, was left to hang his head in shame as he slipped out her door.

<u>Chapter Four</u>

The weeks after the toxicity of her last relationship walked out of her life - and clear out of town - flew by. Though they claimed they weren't rushing things, Lovina and Thomas could barely contain their desire to get married. Before they knew it, the day arrived and people were entering the church. Lovina waited in the bridal chamber, awaiting her aunt to retrieve her. It wasn't a large room, but it was clean and pretty. Something you would imagine would have a likeness to a Victorian sitting room. Lovina smoothed the lines in her skirt down as took a turn around the room. There was a loveseat or fainting couch - it wasn't very large to say the least - two chairs, and a small table. Lovina walked around the room twice before resting upon the couch. As she can't help but smile to herself, Lovina is awoken from her trance by a knock at her door.

"Who is it?"

"It's Deacon Macon, Lovina. May I come in for a moment?"

"Of course," Lovina strides to the door to open it. "What's going on? He's not backing out is he?" Now fearing that she has lost out once again.

"Oh no, nothing of the sort." To that Lovina could breathe a sigh of relief. "I am just here to pass along a message from the groom. Apparently he doesn't think he will have occasion to tell you everything he wants to today and - because he doesn't want to forget - he wrote it down here for you." Deacon Macon extended his hand that held a folded cream piece of paper. Lovina laughed to herself realizing Thomas must have used one of her recipe sheets from the bakery. Taking the paper from Deacon Macon, he bowed out gracefully and left her alone. She sat back down on the loveseat by the window and unfolded the paper before she began to read.

My dearest Lovina,

This is the happiest day of my life. You have done more for me in these few months than I have been able to do for myself in my whole life. I am writing this short dictation to you because I need you to know exactly how I feel if I am unable to speak after I see you walk through the door in mere moments.

I know that we met at a time when you were not feeling like you would ever be happy again, and I want to make sure that you are sure that I am the one who will make you happy forever. I understand at times you may not trust me, you may question me, and you may even be mad at me for something I may not understand. Despite this however, I want you to know that I will not be mad. I will not meet your anger with violence, and I will NOT shame you for feelings you have every right to feel because of how you have been wronged.

I don't mean to bring up unhappy memories on our happy day, but I need you to know that I love you unconditionally, irrevocably, and entirely. I have never felt the kind of love I feel for you, and I can only attest that God must have made me for you and you for me. The only thing I could pray to ask him would be for us to have met sooner so we could have started our life together sooner.

Now, with all that out of the way, this is what I promise to you:

I promise to always love and be with only you.

I promise that whatever children we have, I will love and cherish as much as you.

I promise to raise our children in our faith and our culture to cement their knowledge of our ways.

I promise to take care of my family for as long as I live and even after if I leave before my time.

I promise not to be out late and to help you around the house when I am able.

No matter how old or how weak we grow, I will never leave your side.

Finally, I promise that once a day at least, I will tell you I love you. It may not always be verbally, but whether through a look, through a nod, or an embrace, you will know everyday of our lives together how much I love and will always love you.

Well, I am sure there is more that I am leaving out, but you know I am not very good at typing up a conversation or a letter for that matter… I can't wait to see you and I can't wait to call you my wife.

I love you.

Yours.

Lovina held back tears as she let her hand fall upon her lap. She took her fingers and ran them along the words he wrote to her. Thomas was giving her more than he would ever know, and this note solidifies to her that she will need to make sure she tells him this much and more about how much he means to her.

Life is never simple, nor is it patient and kind. But when you have someone to walk along beside you on this crazy journey, it becomes a bit easier. It isn't an immediate thing, it takes time and effort; but if you are willing to put in the work, someone else will be willing to as well.

AMISH AGAINST THE ODDS

Monica Marks

There was a slight buzzing in her ears but it had been there for the better part of two weeks, something Rachel had grown accustomed to hearing. She knew it wasn't medical but it alarmed her all the same.

It does not take a doctor to see I am blocking outside noise in my own way, she thought ruefully.

It wasn't until Joanna tugged gently on her skirt that she realized someone was trying to get her attention.

"*Mammi*? Bishop Bachman is summoning you."

Rachel glanced down at her small daughter and offered her a quick smile.

"Oh."

She looked toward where Joanna pointed and indeed, the Bishop was waving almost comically for her to join him.

"Come along, *liebchen*," she said to the six-year-old and Joanna followed closely on her mother's heels.

"Lovely service, Bishop," Rachel told the elder without preamble. She did not want to give him a chance to open with platitudes.

He nodded appreciatively and patted Joanna on the head endearingly.

"Did you enjoy it also, little Jo?"

Rachel cringed inwardly, hoping her outspoken child would have something nice to say and to her relief, Joanna nodded eagerly.

"Yes, Bishop Bachman. I like listening to you speak about forgiveness and repentance."

Rachel exhaled slowly, hardly realizing she had been holding her breath.

"They are lessons which we must never forget, regardless of how difficult a time we encounter, right Jo?"

"Yes, Bishop," the child agreed and Rachel tried to ignore the obvious message the Bishop had delivered to her specifically.

"Very good, Jo. Off you go then. I would like to speak with your mother alone."

Rachel stifled a groan. She had intentionally brought Joanna along in hopes that she would not be left to hear the bishop's words of wisdom that afternoon.

"Walk along side me, Rachel," the Bishop ordered and Rachel idly wondered what would happen if she politely refused. It was a fleeting thought, a wicked fantasy rather than something she was apt to do.

She loved Bishop Bachman well. He was a decent man and strong leader. That did not mean she wished to be subjected to his well-meaning advice.

"Of course," she agreed and they headed away from the congregation toward the pond in the middle of the Troyer farm.

"How are you faring these days, Rachel?"

She inadvertently gritted her teeth together and the bishop seemed to catch her expression before she could hide it.

"Rachel, I know this is a trying time for you but I want you to understand you are not alone."

She nodded, trying to force a cheerful smile onto her face but she was certain she was about to dissolve into a puddle of tears if he continued to press her.

"I know," she replied. "I am blessed to have the support of my family and the district."

Bishop Bachman stopped walking and turned to regard her.

"And the Umbels?"

The familiar lump formed quickly, barely giving Rachel enough time to swallow her misery.

She shook her head.

"I do not see much of them but in casual passing," she confessed. The bishop sighed regretfully, his eyes moving toward her in-laws who tried not to stare back at them in the distance. Bishop Bachman returned his gaze to Rachel.

"That is unfortunate but you must understand they feel as badly as you do. It will take time to heal but everyone will get there, *Gotte* willing."

Rachel did not answer, her own eyes shifting back toward where her daughter tagged along after some older children. She purposely avoided looking at the Umbels.

"You already know that your focus must be on Joanna and she seems to be thriving despite the circumstances."

Rachel nodded, her fingers reaching up to play with a strand of honey-blonde hair. It was a nervous habit she had forsaken years earlier but it seemed to have resurfaced in the past weeks.

"Who is helping you on the farm?"

Rachel wondered why he asked questions he already knew the answer to but she dared not voice her own inquiry.

He does not mean any harm. You must not lose your temper with the Bishop.

"I am faring just fine," she fibbed, returning her stare to his concerned eyes. She forced a tight smile onto her lips.

"It is not a big farm, Bishop and I really do not need much to keep it going. Most of my income is from my quilts these days. The farm is secondary."

"Be that as it may, Rachel, you should not be tending to it alone. I will see about having someone help you."

She opened her mouth to protest.

The last thing she wanted was another neighbor prying into the intimate and embarrassing details of what had happened with Eli.

It is not as if they do not already know. They likely knew before I did, she thought bitterly. All Rachel wanted to do was disappear into a world with her daughter and forget the rest of the community.

Overnight it seemed, the life she had cherished in the close-knit Amish district had become a place of alienation and isolation.

The people she had once wanted to share her life with became those to avoid.

"Rachel?" the Bishop pressed. "Will you allow me to find you help?"

She knew there would be no point in arguing with the man. His intentions were good and she knew his worry was genuine.

"That will be fine," she replied. "I should get back to Joanna."

He nodded although Rachel could tell he did not consider the conversation finished.

It is not the last I have heard of this, she thought, sighing silently. *I wonder if I will ever hear the last of this.*

"Hello."

Samuel looked up from the fence post and did a double take as he saw the man standing a few feet away.

"Hello," Samuel replied, rising to his full height. He dropped the hammer in his tool belt and cocked his head to the side, peering at the stranger. He brushed a strand of light brown hair from his face and stared inquisitively at the man.

"Do you work for hire or are you employed by this farmer?"

Samuel's brown eyes narrowed suspiciously.

"I would ask if you were from the IRS but something tells me you aren't," he replied, a slightly sarcastic tone lacing his words.

The stranger chuckled and extended a hand.

"No, you would be correct. I am not from the IRS. My name is Mark Bachman. I am a Bishop with the Amish district just that way. You are?"

Samuel eyed his outstretched palm reluctantly but stepped forward to accept it.

"Samuel Baker."

"Good to meet you, Mr. Baker. I have a member of our district who needs some help on her farm. She has the unfortunate task of tending the land herself, something that happened quite recently. Is this something which might interest you?"

Samuel withdrew his hand and stepped back, his brow knitting in consternation.

"Don't you people help your own?" he asked gruffly. The Bishop seemed amused by his question.

"We try to," he replied. "But sometimes we need outsider assistance. Of course, you would be compensated well for your efforts."

Samuel looked around, wiping the sweat from his neck. He stared at the Bishop, considering the man's words.

Work had been sparse and he had bills to pay. Samuel knew he would be foolish to turn down an offer like that but he could not help but feel suspicious of this bizarre chance encounter.

"How did you come across me?" Samuel demanded. Bishop Bachman pointed at his wagon just down the dirt road.

"I happened to be driving by and I saw you. I have just finished services and I am returning to my home. Truth be told, I think you were a sign from God. I was going to begin looking for help for Rachel in the morning but here you are, working on a Sunday."

Samuel nodded slowly.

"Unfortunately, my bills don't understand days of the week," he muttered and the elder laughed aloud.

"It is one of the many trials and tribulations the English face, I fear. If you were to accept my proposal, you would have Sundays as a day of rest."

Samuel tried to remember a time when any day had been a day of rest.

I haven't rested in years.

So what do you say? Would you be willing to help Rachel on her farm?"

"Is it steady work?"

Samuel wondered why he bothered voicing the question; he was already going to take the job, steady work or not.

"Yes, it is," Bishop Bachman replied. "My guess is for as long as you're willing to do it."

Samuel nodded.

"When does it start?"

"You can begin tomorrow if you are available."

Sam grinned for the first time since meeting the Amish man and extended his palm again.

"I'm available."

"*Mammi,* where did *Daed* go?"

It was not the first time which Joanna had asked the question but it never ceased to send a thousand needles into Rachel's heart.

"Joanna, what have I told you about your father?" she replied, grinding her jaw.

"He has gone away," the child chirped. "But where? And when will he return?"

"He is not coming back!" Rachel's voice was much harsher than she had intended and a look of hurt crossed over her face.

"I am sorry, *Mammi,*" she whispered and Rachel was instantly filled with shame.

She is only a child, longing for her father! You have no cause to snap at her like that!

Rachel extended her arms.

"No, *liebchen,* I am sorry," she gasped, tears springing to her green eyes. "Come here."

Dutifully, Joanna ran into her mother's arms and the two embraced.

"*Daed* is not coming back, not ever," she breathed. "I am sorry to tell you that but you must stop asking about him."

"Why *Mammi?* Why can I not ask about him?"

Rachel bit on her lower lip and buried her face in Joanna's soft blonde mop of hair.

"You must go now, Jo. You will be late for school."

They parted and Jo looked up at her mother.

"Why are you crying, *Mammi?*"

"I only have something in my eye," she fibbed. "Off you go now."

Begrudgingly, Joanna trudged toward the door, glancing back at her mother one last time. Rachel waved encouragingly and painted a smile upon her face.

She is too young to understand any of this. How can I explain it when I barely understand myself.

Rachel sighed and turned back to the sink where she was doing the breakfast dishes.

She had a mountain of work to accomplish that day and she did not know if she would get half of it done. She recalled her conversation with Bishop Bachman the previous day.

I shouldn't be so head strong. I do need help and I should get some assistance before I lose control of the farm. It has only been two weeks and things are already becoming overwhelming.

Rachel reluctantly realized she would be forced to ask her family for help but she knew with their help came an earful of unsolicited advice.

A knock at the front door shattered her thoughts and she glanced back to see Bishop Bachman on the porch.

She waved him inside, drying her hands on her apron.

Ah, speaking of unsolicited advice...

She was immediately filled with contrition.

You should be grateful he cares enough about you to see if you are well.

"*Guder mariye*, Rachel," he called as he entered the small house.

"*Guder mariye*," she replied. "To what do I owe the pleasure, Bishop?"

She hoped he was not about to speak to her about Eli again.

"I have someone whom I would like you to meet," he said as she moved to join him at the entranceway.

Rachel's eyebrows shot up to her hairline.

He cannot mean...

Instantly, Bishop Bachman seemed to read the look of dread on her face.

"It is a handyman," he said quickly and Rachel was filled with a relief so strong, it almost knocked her to her knees.

Of course he would not bring a suitor to my door so soon. Why am I looking at everyone like an enemy?

"Already you have found a handyman?" she replied, surprised. "You must have had someone in mind."

They moved toward the door and the Bishop shook his head.

"No, actually I chanced upon him on the way home yesterday."

As they stepped onto the veranda, Rachel started in shock.

"Rachel Umbel, this is Samuel Baker."

Rachel recovered from her initial reaction immediately stuck her hand out.

"Ah, thank you for coming to my assistance, Mr. Baker," she said quickly, shifting her eyes away from his face.

"No problem," he replied gruffly and Rachel wondered if he had noticed her reaction. They shook hands quickly.

"Tell mc where you want me to go," he said without hesitation and Rachel could sense he was not the conversational type. She found the realization heartwarming.

I will not be forced to entertain him or answer questions all day long, she thought with some happiness.

"Do you have any experience in working with animals? The horses need grooming."

Samuel nodded and looked around, spotting the barn.

Without another word, he disappeared toward the stables, leaving the Bishop and Rachel alone.

"Who is he?" Rachel asked when he was out of earshot. "I have never seen him around the district before."

"As I said, I only just chanced upon him yesterday."

Rachel gnawed on her lower lip, debating whether to ask the obvious question or not.

"What happened to his face?" she finally whispered, her curiosity winning out. The Bishop shrugged.

"I did not think to ask," he replied nonchalantly, turning to leave. "I will be back to pick him up at four o'clock."

Rachel nodded, watching at the Bishop got onto his wagon.

He did not think to ask how that man's face got so horribly disfigured? She thought, shaking her head. *How could he not wish to know?*

Rachel forced the thought of Samuel from her mind and began addressing her long list of chores.

She had her own issues to worry about without bringing in an Englisher's problems also.

Maybe it is time to go back to the city, he thought. *Work is too scarce in Amish country and even if this is steady income, I don't belong here.*

Samuel wondered if he belonged anywhere anymore.

It had been five years since he had called any place "home", wandering from town to town like a nomad. He had no friends, no ties and no money.

At least I will have a better shot of employment in Detroit.

Branch County had been kind to him given his appearance but the thought of returning to the city filled him with a sick which never truly left him.

There was too great a chance he would see Holly in Detroit, no matter where he went.

Detroit has a population of third quarters of a million people. You will not see Holly.

He tried to shove the thought of her from his mind but it seemed her anguished face would forever be etched there.

Maybe in another year, he thought, blinking quickly against his burning lids. *Maybe then I will be able to return to Detroit and face what I have done.*

But he didn't believe himself. It was the same thing he told himself every year around the time of the anniversary.

Sam knew that the pain did not go away, no matter how much he avoided contact with others or hid himself away in the boonies.

It wouldn't happen next near.

He would never go home because home did not exist for him anymore.

The late afternoon sun filtered into the front room and Rachel glanced up suddenly, blinking. She peered down at the quilt she had been sewing and then at the clock in the corner of the room.

How long have I been in here? She thought in shock. She had worked through lunch and her fingers were throbbing.

She had wanted to finish the piece for sale at market on Friday but she had not meant to spend a great deal of time on it, not when there was so much else to be done before Joanna returned from school.

She rose from the rocking chair and peered out the window into the front yard.

And what happened to the Englisher?

A spark of anger coursed through her as she threw open the front door, slightly blinded by the rays. She had not seen him since first thing that morning when she had sent him to groom the horses.

He is probably taking a nap. Why did I agree to let the Bishop bring someone here?

Angrily, she hurried around the back of the house toward the barn and threw open the doors, freezing in her tracks.

The two horses were gleaming and well-groomed in spotless stalls with fresh hay. Samuel had swept out the interior and maintained the unoccupied booths also.

Rachel was sure she had never seen the stables so clean.

She was immediately ashamed for thinking the worst of the Englisher and she looked around to see where he had gone.

If he is napping, he has certainly earned a rest, she thought wryly. *This is more than Eli could accomplish in a day.*

She found Samuel in the garden, weeding through the tomato plants, sweat glistening on his neck and shoulders. There was no sweat on his scarred face and Rachel wondered if he was in constant pain. She certainly hoped not.

She watched him for a moment, touched by his work ethic. No one had guided him to the garden; he had simply taken the task upon himself as he had cleaning out the barn.

"You did good work with the horses," she called out to him. He barely raised his head but he nodded slightly to acknowledge her words.

"Have you taken any water or eaten yet?"

Samuel paused and glanced at her for a moment, seeming unsure of himself. Rachel was struck at how bright brown his eyes seemed through his mangled face and yet she did not find looking at him as unsettling as she had earlier.

Despite his exterior, Rachel could sense a gentleness beneath him, one he seemed to want to keep hidden.

"No, I am fine," he finally answered, turning back to the plants.

"I cannot have you fainting in the sun," Rachel insisted sternly. "Please come in the house for some water at least."

He paused and Rachel reasoned his thirst must have won out in the end.

"All right," he agreed but Rachel thought she heard a slight resentment in his tone.

Silently, he followed her back toward the house and into the side door.

In the kitchen, they didn't speak as Rachel fixed him a glass of lemonade. As she placed the glass before him, she thought he was about to protest but he shut his mouth and took a long sip.

Rachel turned back to the refrigerator.

"I will fix us some lunch," she announced.

"No thank you," Samuel answered quickly. "I should get back to work."

She glanced at him over her shoulder and shook her head.

"You have accomplished more today than I had expected to do all week," she replied. "You can take time for lunch."

Samuel was silent but she could feel him watching her as she made a plate of cheese, bread and fruit.

She set the plate at the table and joined him.

"Do you believe in God?" she asked, glancing at him as he reached for his food. He seemed taken aback by the question.

"I used to," he replied, ripping off a hunk of bread with surprisingly straight teeth. "But he doesn't seem to come around much for me these days."

Rachel nodded and bowed her head.

"Thank you, *Gotte* for sending me help when I needed it most. Please bless our food. Amen."

Samuel dropped his bread and looked embarrassed.

"Amen," he echoed quickly. "I'm sorry. It didn't occur to me to pray."

Rachel smiled and began to eat.

"There is no need to apologize. You are entitled to your beliefs. I did not wish to exclude you if you wished to join," she explained.

Samuel chewed on his morsels slowly, studying her furtively and Rachel sensed that he wanted to say something.

You invited him in to eat. You should encourage him to speak, she thought but in truth, she was rather enjoying the silence of someone who knew nothing about her or her past.

"Did your husband die recently?"

The question was blunt and caught Rachel off guard. She stared at him with clear green eyes, her mouth slightly agape.

Her first instinct was indignation but suddenly, she began to laugh.

"In a way," she replied and Samuel stared at her, his brow raised in surprise at her odd reaction. He did not question her further.

"I am sorry for your loss," he muttered, fixating his eyes on the table. "It is not easy to lose someone you love."

Rachel was moved by his tone and despite her resolve not to engage in conversation, she found herself intrigued by the hardworking stranger.

"Are you married?" she asked.

"Not anymore."

He is as vague as I am, she thought, partly amused, partly annoyed. She wondered if he was simply treating her the way she was treating him.

Do unto others...

"You are very good around the farm," she told him. "Do you have a farm of your own?"

He shook his head.

"No," he replied. "I grew up on one though, before I moved to Michigan."

The sound of hooves approaching the house caused them to glance out of the window and suddenly Rachel saw Joanna skip around the side of the property.

"My daughter is home," she said, rising and dusting the crumbs from her apron as Joanna came slipping through the door. "But I can't see who has come by wagon."

"*Mammi*, Bishop Bachman is - "

Joanna turned to stone as she took in the stranger in her kitchen. Her small face became a mask of fear as she stared at Samuel, her mouth open with fear.

Terrified that Joanna would say something impolite, Rachel piped up immediately.

"Joanna, this is Mr. Baker. He will be helping us on the farm. Samuel, this is my daughter Joanna."

She nudged her daughter gently but Joanna could not seem to overcome her horror of Samuel's scarred face and hid her eyes in her mother's skirt.

Rachel turned apologetically to Samuel.

"I am sorry," she started. "She's shy – "

It was at that moment that she realized Samuel's face was a statue still as Joanna's had been. He gaped at the girl, his fierce eyes wide with an emotion Rachel could not place.

"Samuel, are you all right?" Rachel asked.

"Hello? Rachel? Are you here?" Bishop Bachman called, entering the house through the front door. The elder's voice seemed to shatter Samuel's trance-like state.

"I didn't know you had a daughter," Samuel mumbled, spinning to leave. "I – I'm sorry. I can't come back here."

He disappeared from the kitchen, almost barreling over Bishop Bachman who appeared in the doorway. The bishop's smile faded as he watched Samuel run out the door toward his wagon.

"What happened? Did it go badly today?" he demanded but Rachel had no answer for him.

She pulled Joanna close to her, her heart racing.

"*Mammi,* is that man a monster?" Joanna whispered.

"Dear *Gotte*, I hope not, *liebchen*," Rachel murmured in response.

The fire raged hot and terrifying. Joanna's screams could scarcely be heard above the popping of the wood beams and Rachel raced about looking for her daughter.

"Joanna!" she cried, tears streaking down her face. "Joanna, where are you?"

But the child only continued to shriek and Rachel tried to find her despite the billowing, blinding smoke encasing the barn.

She saw a movement out of the corner of her eye and suddenly, Samuel emerged, holding Joanna, limp in his arms, his eyes wild.

Rachel began to howl.

Rachel started awake, her body drenched in sweat.

Without hesitation, she slipped from her bed and rushed into Joanna's room, pushing open the door in fear.

The child lay sleeping peacefully, her body half curled with a soft smile on her face.

Slowly, Rachel's breath steadied but she could not bring herself to leave the room and she slid quietly onto the single mattress beside her daughter.

She could not forget the crazed expression in Samuel's eyes from her dream.

Who did I allow into my house? She thought, willing herself to be calm.

It did not matter; he would not be back.

For some inexplicable reason, the reality of that filled Rachel with sadness.

As dawn broke, Rachel had not slept again and reluctantly she left Joanna's side to make breakfast.

There was a darkness to the day and Rachel sensed they were in for rain.

It will be a good day to work on my quilts, she thought and immediately she was grateful for the work that Samuel had done on the farm the previous day. Losing a day to bad weather was something she could not afford in her position.

Confusion filled her.

How can I be thankful he helped and fear him also?

She was beginning to wonder if the dream had not been a warning but something else.

It is irrelevant now. Samuel is gone and you must find someone else to help on the farm.

Sighing, she continued to fix the morning meal and Joanna eventually slipped downstairs.

"*Guder mariye, Mammi,*" the child chirped, slipping onto a chair.

"Hello, *liebchen.* Did you sleep well?"

Joanna nodded.

"I had a wonderful dream," she told her mother, her bright green eyes wide.

"What did you dream of?"

"The Englisher from yesterday," she replied and Rachel stared at her in shock.

"What of him?" she demanded, her face growing hot with worry.

"He brought me to a field with flowers, all with many colors and tall grasses. There was another little girl there too. He told me her name was Brittany. She and I skipped and played, picking flowers and praying together. And you know what *Mammi*?"

Unexpected tears filled Rachel's eyes.

"What, Jo?"

"The Englisher's face was not scarred. He was pleasant to look at."

Rachel's voice caught in her throat.

We both dreamt of him last night but very different dreams. I wonder what it means.

"Eat your breakfast, *liebchen*."

Joanna nodded agreeably, leaving Joanna to her thoughts.

Samuel lay on his bed, unable to move as memories consumed him, filling him with devastation and pain.

I reacted very badly yesterday, he thought, his heart heavy but he could not bring himself to move. *I will never be able to overcome this. I will be haunted by Brittany and Holly until I die.*

Seeing Joanna Umbel had stirred something in him which he had tried to supress for years but he should have known it would rear its ugly head at the most inopportune time.

Now I have alarmed Rachel and ruined the only chance I have had for steady employment in such a long time.

There was more to it, something Samuel did not want to admit to himself.

He was strangely drawn to Rachel, despite her somewhat standoffish nature.

Maybe that is why I am drawn to her, he reasoned. *She is not pushy or intrusive. She leaves me alone but she seems caring. I wonder what happened to her husband.*

There was a knock on the door to his basement apartment and Samuel made no move to answer it.

"Samuel? It's Bishop Bachman."

Sam groaned inwardly, cursing himself for allowing the bishop to know where he lived.

"Bishop, I thought I told you I'm not going back to the Umbel farm," he yelled from his spot on his cot.

"Yes, but I would like to speak with you for a moment. Please, Samuel, it's raining outside."

Sam rolled his eyes but reluctantly rose to let the older man inside.

It wasn't very godly to leave him standing in the water after all.

"Come in," he muttered begrudgingly, stepping aside for Bishop Bachman to enter. The elder removed his hat, droplets of water falling to the entranceway. He looked at Samuel apologetically.

"I am sorry to bother you so early, Samuel but I wanted to stop by and see if you had changed your mind."

Sam shook his head quickly.

"No," he replied flatly. "But thanks for checking in."

"May I ask what happened?"

Sam peered at him questioningly.

"Are you people always like this?"

The bishop seemed genuinely tickled even though Samuel had meant to sound gruff.

"If you mean do we always take care of one another then the answer is yes."

A foreign pang of appreciation sparked through Sam as he stared at the man.

"I am going to be frank with you, Samuel. Rachel is going through a very difficult time. Her husband shamed her family and the community by leaving with another woman. He has been shunned and it is not something that we take lightly. Unfortunately, Rachel has found herself feeling isolated also. She does not wish to seek counsel and I cannot say that I am surprised she has retreated into herself. I have grown concerned for her."

Samuel was shocked by the revelation.

What kind of idiot leaves a woman like that? He thought angrily. His mind went to Joanna and he swallowed a lump in his throat.

What kind of man leaves behind a beautiful daughter when he is so blessed to have one?

"When I saw you working the other day, I got the impression that you, too, enjoy your solitude. Am I mistaken?" Bishop Bachman continued.

Sam chuckled somewhat mirthlessly.

"As a rule, yes," he replied. The bishop nodded understandingly.

"I felt that your presence might be beneficial to Rachel, both from a work standpoint but also as a silent support to her. Honestly, I am surprised that you two did not get along better."

Samuel did not respond but suddenly the Bishop's unexpected approach made sense.

He saw a damaged man and he matched me with a damaged woman.

Samuel was unsure how to feel about it.

"I will not keep you, Samuel but if you should happen to change your mind, I am certain that Rachel could still use the assistance...and the companionship."

Bishop Bachman turned to leave.

"Wait a minute," Sam called after him. "I thought you Amish didn't like outsiders."

The older man turned to smile enigmatically.

"Perhaps you will not always be an outsider, Samuel. Perhaps there is a place for you in this world with us."

The idea was stunning and he watched the Bishop replace his hat, disappearing into the rain.

Did he just suggest that I join the Amish? That is crazy.

But long after Bishop Bachman left, Samuel could not shake the spark of hope which had been ignited in his belly.

How long had it been since he belonged somewhere?

The buzzing in her ears was louder than usual that morning and it did not seem to lessen no matter how Rachel tried to distract herself.

Suddenly, it seemed accompanied by a roar and her heart racing, she wondered if there was something terribly wrong.

It was not until she peered out the front window did she realize that an auto had pulled up to the farm.

Her jaw dropped suddenly as she recognized Samuel jump from the driver's seat and hurry through the rain toward the door.

Joanna had already left for school and Rachel was alone in the house, working on her quilt.

What is he doing here? She wondered but there was no fear in his arrival. If anything, she felt a slight excitement.

"Did you forget something?" she asked, staring at him quizzically as stepped onto the front porch.

"Yes," he replied. "I forgot my manners."

She eyed him in confusion.

"Your manners?" she echoed. He shrugged sheepishly and Rachel realized that he was wet despite the short distance from the car to the door.

"Come in," she urged. "I will make coffee."

Am I making a mistake allowing him inside? She wondered but in her heart, she could not reconcile Samuel Baker with darkness.

He was a man in pain, that much was clear but why?

"Thanks," he told her, sitting at the kitchen table. "Listen, I thought about it and I know I probably scared you when I left yesterday."

Rachel glanced at him.

"It was abrupt, yes," she replied diplomatically. She did not tell him about her nightmare even though it had been plaguing her all day.

"I owe you an explanation," he said.

She placed two cups of coffee on the table, offering cream and sugar before sitting across from him, ready to listen.

He stared at her for a long moment and Rachel could sense that he was gathering his courage to put the words together.

Exhaling, he started.

"Once, a long time ago, I had a successful landscaping company in Detroit. I had clients in the suburbs and I did very well. I was married. My wife's name was Holly and we had a daughter."

Rachel felt her heart begin to race as she studied his face.

"One night, I came home from work, exhausted. Holly wanted to go out with friends and she left me alone with our daughter. I put her to bed and made myself something to eat."

Samuel stopped talking, his voice choked with emotion.

"I must have fallen asleep because when I opened my eyes, the house was on fire. Flames were licking my face but all I could think about was my baby girl. I raced toward the stairs, unaware of the burns and the blisters..."

Rachel's hand flew to her mouth and she gasped.

"There were no stairs left. There was no way to the second floor. The firefighters dragged me from the house, screaming in pain but not from the charred flesh. Holly stood in the night, staring at me and I will never forget the look on her face."

Samuel hung his head. Rachel could see him visibly shaking.

"She never forgave me. How could she? Brittany was dead because of me."

"It was an accident," Rachel murmured. "You did everything you could."

Samuel shook his head.

"No, I didn't. I couldn't take the aftermath. The guilt ate me alive. I filed for a divorce even though Holly needed me to mourn the loss of our daughter. I ran and I could never go back."

Rachel could not stop the tears from falling down her cheeks, trying to imagine the loss of her child.

"How can anyone be expected to handle such a situation well?" she asked quietly. Samuel laughed shortly.

"I heard she has remarried and had another child since. She has moved on. It seems I am the only one stuck in limbo."

Suddenly Rachel remembered Joanna's dream.

"Joanna dreamt about Brittany last night," she whispered. Samuel's head jerked up and his eyes narrowed slightly.

"Is that supposed to make me feel better?"

Rachel shook her head quickly, growing excited.

"No, she did. She told me the little girl in her dream was named Brittany and she saw you before the accident."

Samuel regarded her.

"Maybe Bishop Bachman was right," he mumbled, looking at his hands in embarrassment.

"What did he say?" she asked curiously.

"He thinks that God brought us together."

Their eyes met and a slow smile formed on Rachel's mouth.

"Please never repeat this to him," she whispered, taking Samuel's hand. "But Bishop Bachman is rarely wrong."

Samuel squeezed her palm gently.

"I look forward to learning that for myself," he replied.

As if his words were the anecdote, the humming in Rachel's ears subsided.

She could hear clearly again.

HANNAH'S DILEMMA

95

ELIZA BAKER

Part One:

"Two more are gone."

Hannah King kept her eyes trained on the dough she was kneading on the butcher block counter in front of her. Her daed spoke in a low voice to her maemm as the two stood by the back door, and Hannah knew that they didn't want her to hear what they were saying. But she couldn't help but eavesdrop. She knew that they were talking about two more cows being gone. That made it the fourth theft in less than a month.

At first it had only been one cow here or there. No one had noticed at first, but when her daed's prize bull went missing, the family realized that something was wrong. Other families in the neighborhood had also been struck. The men were still trying to figure out how to catch the thief or thieves, but whoever was responsible seemed to be two steps ahead.

"No," Hannah's maemm gasped. "How can this be, Richard?"

Glancing over her shoulder, Hannah saw her daed shrug. The weariness on his face made Hannah's heart break. Who could be doing this to them? She had to believe that it was an Englischer who had a grudge against her family or the community in general. It certainly couldn't be one of their own people. That was absurd.

Hannah looked back to her bread dough before either of her parents caught her watching them. She didn't want to make them feel worse than they already did. Without their prize bull, they needed to raise the money to buy a new one. And Hannah had no idea how that would happen. Normally they would ask the bishop of their church district to dip into the community fund to help them out, but so many people had been hit by the thieves that there wouldn't be enough money to help everyone. Besides, Hannah was fairly certain that her parents didn't want to take money that others needed more.

When her maemm gave a shuddering sigh, Hannah decided that once the bread was rising, she was going to take a prayer walk. She had taken to praying while she took her daily walk, and now she craved the time alone with the Lord. Today she needed the time more than ever because she had a specific prayer request to make: she needed to find a way to help her family.

A moment later her maemm joined her back at the butcher block counter. Hannah glanced up at her quickly, and she could see that her mother had been crying. She was still trying to hold back the tears. Hannah knew that her maemm wasn't going to share with her, so she bit back her questions.

With a final roll of the dough, Hannah was satisfied that she had kneaded the bread thoroughly enough. "Maemm?" she asked. "Would you mind if I went for a walk? I'll be back in plenty of time to finish the bread for supper."

"What? Oh, *da,* of course you can go. Enjoy the nice weather." Her maemm didn't even look up from the vegetables she was chopping as she waved Hannah out of the house.

Hannah washed her hands at the pump sink, straightened her kapp, and hurried out the back door. She saw her daed and her brothers in a circle over by the barn, and she knew that he was telling them about the most recent theft. Her heart cramped in her chest, and she turned away to hurry toward her path in the woods that bordered her family's farm.

Lord, Hannah prayed, *I don't know why this is our cross to bear at the moment, but it is. I can accept that I can't have all the answers right now, but we need your help, Lord. How can I help my family earn more money so that we can replace the livestock that we have lost? How do I convince my parents to let me help? I'm listening, Lord. Amen.*

Wind rustled the leaves of the trees, so Hannah paused. She had learned that the signs of the Lord's presence were all around her if only she would listen. No answers came to her immediately, but she felt peace wash over her so she kept walking.

The trail wound through thick stands of trees as it followed the creek that meandered through the valley that separated her family's farm from that of her beau, Abram. Just thinking about him now sent a flush creeping up her neck. The two had been sweethearts since they were children, and she assumed that eventually the two would marry. Lately, though, he had seemed...distant...almost secretive.

No, she was just being silly, she told herself. She brushed off her concerns, and tried to concentrate on listening to an answer to her questions. Once she'd started thinking about Abram, though, she found that she was too distracted to focus.

A branch snapped to her right, and Hannah froze. There weren't any wild animals that she needed to be worried about. Still, she turned toward the sound, watching, and waiting warily. Another branch snapped, and Hannah felt uneasy for a moment.

"Abram!" she exclaimed as her beau stepped out from behind the trees. Her breath caught in her chest, but she was glad to see him.

"Hannah," Abram said, a frown creasing his forehead as he saw her. She returned his frown. Why didn't he seem happy to see her? "What are you doing out here?"

"Just taking a walk," she said, still frowning at him. "I have a lot to think about, to pray about."

"You should be careful," he said, nodding once before he reached toward her. He pulled her into a quick hug before setting her on her path toward home. "I'll come by later."

And with that he disappeared back into the trees.

Part Two:

The next morning Hannah woke up with a headache. Her maemm and daed had sat all of them down the night before to tell them about the most recent cattle thefts. Hannah had to pretend that she didn't know what they were talking about, but every now and then she had glanced at her brothers and sisters, who all seemed genuinely shocked. She couldn't blame them. After the last set of thefts, the local sheriff had seemed to think that he had caught the person who was responsible. This latest theft proved that theory wrong.

"I don't understand," Mary said. Hannah turned toward her sister who was only eleven months younger than her. The two of them often thought alike, but Mary often said what was on her mind, where Hannah kept her mouth shut, content to watch and listen. Now she was curious to hear what her sister had to say. Mary continued, "The sheriff said that he caught the man responsible, so does this mean that someone else is now stealing our cattle or that they didn't get the right person?"

Their daed shook his head slowly, and Hannah couldn't help but notice how weary he looked as he told them all that he simply didn't have any good answers for them.

Now as Hannah slowly sat up in bed, she realized that Abram had never come by last night. She wondered what had kept him, but she couldn't use up her brain space wondering about that. She still hadn't gotten the answer to her prayers that she had been seeking, and now in the bright morning light, she wondered if that was because she had gotten distracted during her prayer time yesterday. Was the lack of an answer a punishment for not being faithful enough? Hannah knew that she needed to get her chores done so she could get outside to go for another prayer walk.

Hurrying to dress, Hannah noticed that Mary had already awoken. Hannah wondered if her sister had the same sense of urgency to figure out how to help their parents out of this situation. "I'll feed the chickens, Maemm," Hannah called as she whirled through the kitchen.

"No need," her maemm said, halting Hannah's progress as she reached out her hand to the back door. "Mary's already done that. If you could start the eggs for breakfast that would be wonderful."

Hannah didn't hesitate to pull out the large, chipped ceramic bowl that they used to stir the eggs in when they made scrambled eggs for breakfast. After she had cracked twelve eggs, Hannah added some heavy cream that had been brought in from their milk cow, Daisy. That was Hannah's not-so-secret secret for making perfect eggs. She added some salt and pepper before taking the whisk, and beating air into them until the yolks looked light and fluffy.

"Do you mind if I go for a walk after my chores are done?" Hannah asked.

"As long as you are back by dinner time," her maemm answered.

Hannah took the cast iron skillet to the stove, and made the eggs while the rest of her siblings drifted into the kitchen, some fresh in from their morning chores. While they sat down to eat, Hannah's mind drifted to Abram's absence once again. She couldn't help but wonder if something had happened to their cattle. The thought made Hannah's stomach tighten with worry. She would have to stop over there after her prayer walk. Her leg jiggled as she felt her impatience rise. When had her family become such slow eaters?

"Daughter, what is wrong with you this morning? You look like a cat dropped in a bucket of water," her daed said.

Blinking at him in surprise, Hannah shook her head as she flushed. "No, I'm fine. I apologize," she said. "I didn't sleep well. I'm just looking forward to getting outside to tend the garden."

Her daed studied her for a long moment before he nodded. "I heard that Abram has been looking to start his own herd of cattle," he remarked.

Hannah's flush deepened at the implication of that statement. She looked at her plate of eggs and sausage. "I don't know about any of that," she told her family before anyone else could say anything.

"I heard that Abram's daed lost four sheep yesterday," Benjamin announced between forkfuls of egg.

At that news, Hannah's head snapped up. That must have been the reason that Abram hadn't come over last night. She should go over to console the family. Up until now, Abram's family had avoided falling victim to the thefts. Their sheep herd was prized in the community, and

Abram's daed had spent his whole life building the herd to be what it was.

It took everything in her to keep her leg still as she finished her breakfast. After everyone had finished eating, Mary offered to help her wash up. When the two of them were alone, Mary asked, "Do you think that Abram is going to propose soon?"

"How should I know?" Hannah asked, feeling the flush rise up her cheeks again. "We haven't really talked about that."

Mary arched an eyebrow. "You've been together for years."

"Oh, fine, we've talked about getting married, and I assume it will happen, but it will have to happen when he's ready," Hannah said. "And if his family has been affected by the thefts, then I don't know when that will be."

Part Three:

Taking a deep breath, Hannah walked up the driveway that led to Abram's house. Her stomach was in knots, and she didn't know how she was going to ask him to help, especially if his own family was now hurting from the rash of thefts. The answer to her prayers had come to her as she had hurried over to Abram's house after she had finished her chores

As she walked she had prayed a quick prayer that she knew wasn't her best one. *Dear Lord,* she prayed, *I know that I'm not praying as deeply as I should, but I need your help. How do I help my family out of this mess? Amen.*

Before she had even had the chance to knock on the front door, it swung open, and Abram's younger sister, Lucy, launched herself at Hannah in a full throttle hug. "Hannah! I haven't seen you in ages," the younger girl cried with delight.

Hannah hugged her back, and couldn't help but chuckle. "Is Abram home?" she asked as Lucy dragged her inside.

"Oh, he's out back helping daed count the sheep. Daed actually thought that four of the sheep had been stolen like all those cattle! Can you believe that?" Lucy exclaimed.

"They weren't?" Hannah asked, confusion slipping through her resolve to ask Abram for help.

"No, they were just lost in the south pasture," Lucy said as she shook her head. "They really caused quite a stir, though. Daed said that your folks lost some more cattle. I'm really sorry about that, Hannah. Do you think they'll ever catch the guy?"

Hannah felt the weight of her family's situation crash down on her, but she did her best to pull a brave smile up on her face. "I sure hope so," she said.

"Sit here and I'll go get the cookies I made this morning," Lucy said, and before Hannah could say anything else, Lucy had disappeared into the kitchen.

Hannah wanted to call after her that really she just wanted to see Abram. The stress of her family's situation was weighing on her so heavily that she needed to share it with someone. She felt God's call before she could put words to it, and in an instant she knew that she needed to share it with the Lord first and foremost.

So while Lucy was still puttering around in the kitchen Hannah bowed her head, and began to pray. *Dear Lord, I'm sorry for my lack of humility. Forgive me for my stupidity. My heart is aching for my parents and for my family. I need your help to bear this cross. I know that you will keep us safe, and guide us through this storm. Amen.*

She finished her prayer just as Lucy came in with a plateful of cookies. A feeling of peace descended on her, and even though she didn't have any more answers than she had started with, she was able to eat a few of the sugar cookies without feeling the need to rush through the visit. Lucy did most of the talking, and Hannah listened with a smile tugging the corners of her mouth.

When they had finished, Hannah stood, and dusted her crumb covered hands on her apron. "I'm just going to pop out back to say hello to Abram. You should stop by our house soon," Hannah told Lucy. "Mary's been making some chocolate chip cookies that you would love"

Slipping through the always warm kitchen, Hannah said hello to Abram's maemm before she stepped out onto the back porch. From where she stood she could see the whole of the farm with the big milking barn and the horse barn, and the small sheds that housed the chickens and goats. Beyond all of that was the large barn that housed the sheep. Green fields spread out in every direction butting up against the woods that separated Abram's family farm from her own family's farm.

She was still looking at the beauty of the farm when she caught sight of Abram and his daed coming out of the barn. They looked like they were deep in conversation so she waited until there seemed to be a lull in their conversation before she waved and called, "Abram!"

Abram turned, and she thought that she saw a frown flit across his handsome features before he waved her toward them. Hannah tried to shake off her moment of unease, before she hurried over. Abram's daed greeted her before he headed back into the house.

"I missed you yesterday," Hannah said.

"Yeah, I'm sorry about that," Abram said. "My daed thought that some of his sheep had been stolen so I had to go out searching for them in the dark. We found them eventually, but it was still a long night."

Something flashed through the edge of Hannah's mind, but she couldn't pin it down. "My daed lost more cattle last night," Hannah said with a sigh.

"I heard about that this morning," Abram said, glancing back at the barn, seeming distracted. "I'm sorry about that."

A bawling cry from the back of the barn drew their attention, and Hannah stepped toward it. Through the dimly lit interior of the barn she could see several calves on the other side. Before she could ask Abram about it, he was already guiding her away.

Still distracted, Hannah blurted, "Abram, you have to help us. How will my family survive all these thefts? We can't afford a new bull."

An uncomfortable look crossed Abram's face, and that discomfort made the thought flit through Hannah's mind again. Something about the way Abram had been so distant lately, and now the way he was shuffling her away from the barn and toward the path home.

"Listen," he said. "I have some things that my daed needs me to attend to, but I promise that I'll stop by later."

And once again, he strode off without another backward glance.

Part Four:

She couldn't believe that she was actually beginning to think that Abram could have anything to do the thefts. Still, as she hurried down the path through the woods, tears blurring her vision, all she could think about were the five new calves in the back stall of the barn. Where had he gotten them? A purchase like that would be big news throughout their community.

Tears burned the backs of her eyes. She had spent so many years assuming that she and Abram would be married and start a family together that she had missed the part where they were growing apart. But had they? Were they? The questions pounded at her temples as she moved faster through the woods.

By the time she got home, she was more confused than ever. Not wanting to let her family see her crying, Hannah made her way to the horse barn where she climbed up into the hay loft. No one would think to look for her there.

The sweet smelling hay surrounded her like a cloud, hiding her away from the rest of the world. The problems that had been swirling around her seemed to drift away for a few moments. When she was a little girl she had come up here after fights with friends or sisters, and when she could spend a few minutes alone with God, she felt better.

God, where are you? She prayed quietly. She didn't want to be a person who lost her faith just because of hardship or strife, but suddenly she felt overwhelmed by the enormity of the situation that she and her family were facing.

Rustling at the foot of the ladder caused Hannah to prop herself up on her elbows. Mary's concerned face popped up over the side of the hayloft floor. Hannah allowed herself to flop back down on to the hay.

"Are you okay?" Mary asked. "I saw you make a beeline over here when you came out of the woods. I thought you might need some company."

Mary climbed into the hay with her, and settled down. The two lay in silence for a long while, and Hannah appreciated her sister's ability to understand her moods. Finally Hannah said, "Do you think that anything will be okay?"

"I'm not sure what exactly you are talking about, but if it's about the cattle thefts, I think it's going to be really hard for maemm and daed to recover. Daed might have to try to find outside work again." Mary paused. "That's not all that you are talking about is it?"

Hannah sighed. "No, it's not. Can I tell you something?"

"Of course," Mary said, propping herself up on her elbow.

"But you can't tell anyone," Hannah said. She took a deep breath. "I think that maybe Abram is involved in the thefts somehow."

"Don't be ridiculous," Mary said. "This is Abram we're talking about."

"He's been so distant lately," Hannah said, barreling on. "And there are at least four new calves in his barn."

Mary got quiet at that news, but she shook her head. "I still think that you aren't seeing the situation clearly. I don't mean to be rude about it, but how can you even think that about Abram. Don't you love him?"

"Of course I do!" Hannah exclaimed, feeling her heart squeeze in her chest.

"Then, I don't understand, how can you suspect him of something so awful?" Mary asked.

Hannah blinked up at the barn's high ceiling. Her sister had a good point. How could she? "I can't explain it," she said. "Even though I love him with all my heart, I guess I've just been looking for an answer so hard that I was willing to see signs everywhere I looked. I was imposing my own will instead of letting God's will be done. I'll have to make a confession before the bishop."

The sisters fell silent again for a long time. "So what are you going to do?" Mary finally asked.

"I don't know," Hannah said. Sitting up, she brushed hay off her dress. "But I'm going to pray about it. And this time, I'm really going to listen with my whole heart."

Part Five:

The darkness pressed in on her, and Hannah pulled her shawl tighter around herself. Hannah knew that she was on a fool's errand, and that she was probably putting herself in harm's way, but she couldn't see any other way. At worst Abram might be involved in the thefts, and at best he had simply been unwilling to help.

She held the flashlight that she had pulled out of her daed's tool chest in the barn, but she was determined not to turn it on until it was absolutely necessary. The moon lent a faint glow to the path around the far pasture, but Hannah was determined to stay near the fence. If she followed the weathered wooden rails, then she knew she wouldn't get lost.

Somewhere in the distance a cow called out, sounding startled. Hannah paused, listening hard for other noises. Hearing nothing, she continued her trek around the pasture fence. When she had thought this plan through she had figured that the best place to watch and wait for the cattle thieves was down by the gate that was closest to the main road. She just hadn't figured out how hard it would be to get over there.

"What do you think you're doing?"

Hannah stifled a scream as she spun around to see Mary carrying a lantern coming up behind her. "Mary! What are you doing here?" Hannah asked in a hushed, exasperated whisper.

"That's exactly what I am asking you," Mary retorted, propping her hand on her hip. The lantern in her other hand bobbed and swung precariously.

"Blow that out," Hannah said, lunging toward her sister. "What if they see it?"

"Who?" Mary asked as she moved the lantern out of her sister's way.

"The cattle thieves," Hannah said. "That's why I'm out here. I want to prove once and for all that Abram isn't involved in this mess, and at the same time find out who is responsible so that we can get our cattle back."

Even in the dim moonlight Hannah could see Mary looking at her in disbelief. "I don't think that's such a good idea," she finally said.

Hannah laughed, and then clapped a hand over her mouth. She looked around quickly. Seeing no one, she turned her attention back to her younger sister. "It's too late for that now," she said. "I need to see this through. I just...I have to know. I hope you can understand that."

"I don't understand," Mary admitted, "but that doesn't affect the fact that I will support you no matter what. I'll come with you. There's strength in numbers after all."

Hannah felt a surge of warmth and love toward her sister. "Thank you," she whispered. "Now the plan is to go around the perimeter of the fence until we get to the gate that leads to the main road. I figure that's the most likely place to see if the cattle thieves come tonight."

As they walked forward Mary asked, "And then what?"

"Honestly, I don't know," Hannah admitted.

"Why do you think they'll come here tonight?" Mary asked.

"I don't know that they'll come here tonight, but I am planning to it here every night until they do come back," Hannah said with more confidence than she felt.

Mary propped her hand on her hip, and sighed. "And then what?" she repeated. "Hannah, if you are going to come up with a harebrained plan, then you have to think it all the way through."

"Actually I'm not sure that I do need to think it all the way through," Hannah said, pressing her lips together to suppress a smile, despite the fact that her sister wouldn't be able to see it anyway. "The definition of harebrained allows me to only think through the first part."

"Hannah, really," Mary said with such exasperation that Hannah couldn't help but giggle. Even in the strange circumstances she found herself in, her sister still made her laugh. "Actions have consequences."

"I know that actions have consequences," Hannah snapped. "But this was all I could think of. Do you have a better suggestion?"

Mary spread out her hands. "I think it's a little late for that, don't you?"

"Well, then you have two choices, you can either stay with me and see what happens, or you can go back home," Hannah said, wrapping her hand around the flashlight before she turned away. I don't have any more choices. I have to find out who is trying to ruin our family, and I need to clear Abram's name."

"Well, obviously I have to come with you," Mary said. "I couldn't live with myself if I went home and then something happened to you."

Hannah nodded, but didn't say anything as she began walking again. Despite the fact that she had been all bluster when suggesting that her sister return to the house, Hannah was secretly glad that her sister was coming with her. There was always safety in numbers...though Hannah wasn't sure that either of them would be safe if they ended up coming face to face with the cattle thieves.

When the two got to the end of the fence, Hannah instinctively dropped down into a crouch. She yanked down her sister, and motioned for Mary to be quiet. Hannah wasn't sure what had caused her to feel like the two of them were threatened, but she knew, she just knew, that there was something out there that made her alert.

A flash of light from the opposite side of the road, near the woods, made Mary gasp beside her, and Hannah gripped her sister's arm. In her mind she was telling herself that they needed to remain quiet, but her body ignored her brain.

Clutching the flashlight in her hand, Hannah let go of her sister, and leapt to her feet. With her heart pounding in her throat, she shouted, "You! Over there! Stop where you are! I know what you are doing, and I'm not going to let you get away with it!"

Part Six:

"Hannah?"

The sound of total disbelief in Abram's voice made her stomach cramp. She should have known that her discovery was too good to be true. For one triumphant moment, Hannah had been sure that she had caught the cattle thieves. Even as her mind had scrambled to figure out what to do next, she had been thrilled to think that she had finally solved her family's problem. Her heart was beating so hard in her chest that she thought it might break right in front of Abram.

"Yes, it's me," Hannah replied, trying—and failing—to keep the tears out of her voice.

"What are you doing out here?" Abram asked, still sounding confused.

"I could ask the same of you," Hannah said, pushing her broken heart aside. She was going to put an end to this once and for all.

Abram took a step toward her, and Hannah instinctively took a step back. She hated that this was how she was acting with the man she loved—-and she did still love him dearly—but all the evidence that she had at her disposal pointed to Abram being the culprit.

"It isn't safe for you to be out here," Abram said, stepping closer.

"Why?" Hannah asked. She needed him to tell her the truth, even if it wasn't something that she wanted to hear.

"If the cattle thieves show up again—" Abram was cut off by the sound of an engine revving in the distance. Swiftly, he grabbed the flashlight out of her hand, clicked it off, and pulled her down below the fence line so that they wouldn't be seen.

Hannah's heart began to pound in her chest, and her temples began to throb as she realized that even though she didn't know exactly what was going on, she had her evidence that Abram wasn't involved. But, then, why was he out here so late at night?

When she asked him that exact question, she could feel him grimace. "I should be asking you the same thing," he muttered. "But I'm out here as part of a community patrol that your daed set up. We've been watching for the cattle thieves at different farms for weeks, but so far we haven't been able to catch them."

Hannah's cheeks flamed with embarrassment and shame. "Abram, I have something to tell you," she said softly.

"What? Are you going to confess that you're one of the cattle thieves?" he asked.

The humor in his voice only made the situation worse. Taking a deep breath, Hannah said, "I thought you might be involved. In the thefts, I mean. I don't know why. Well, maybe I do. I was so worried about my family that I was looking for an answer wherever I could see one. I'm so sorry. When you started to get distant, I didn't know what to think. And I thought the worst. I understand if you are angry with me. And I understand if you never want to see me again."

To her amazement, Abram burst out in laughter that he quickly stifled. "I don't mean to laugh at you," he said with all the seriousness he could muster. "But why didn't you just come to me with your concerns? We could have cleared all this up, and you wouldn't have had to feel the need to come out in the middle of the night to stalk dangerous cattle thieves."

"You're still teasing me," Hannah pointed out, although she was beginning to feel herself relax.

"Maybe just a little," Abram admitted. "But only because you seem so upset."

"Well, I thought that you might be destroying my family's livelihood, so I think that it will take a moment longer before I feel cheerful again," Hannah said. She heard the distress still in her voice, creeping out as she spoke.

"It does hurt that you would think that of me," Abram said after a long moment of silence. "But I can understand that you needed to put the pieces together."

Hannah stepped forward, and reached out to take Abram's hand. "I am sorry that I suspected you," she said. "But I'm sorrier that I didn't come talk to you about my concerns. Well...I did try one day, but you and your daed were busy, and then I saw the calves, and well..."

"You saw the calves?" Abram's voice sounded choked and higher than normal. "You weren't supposed to see the calves."

Another shot of fear went through Hannah's stomach. Could it be that Abram was still somehow involved in the cattle thievery? Could he be lying to her? She thought through the conversation that they had just had, and she decided that she knew Abram. She knew his heart, and she had been praying for answers. She loved him, and she knew that she had been wrong to doubt him. She still had a lot of questions, though, and she knew that she needed to be bold to ask him.

"I saw the calves," she confirmed. "What were they for Abram? How did you find the money to buy four calves? I thought...I thought that you were saving for our future."

Abram sighed, and dropped Hannah's hand so he could run both hands through his hair. In the dim light of the glow from the flashlight, she could see the hair sticking up in all different directions. She thought that he looked as frazzled as she felt.

"They were, are, for our future," Abram said. "The calves, I mean. They are for our future. I took out a loan from my daed to buy them. I'm going to raise them, sell them, and after I pay back my daed, buy some more. I just thought that it would be better to make a small profit before I told you about them, but I can see now that I should have shared my thoughts with you."

"That would have been nice," Hannah agreed. "But I guess I can see why you did that."

A silence descended upon them, but Hannah still had other questions. She still had other thoughts that she needed to share with him, but she knew that now wasn't the time for a long conversation. Suddenly she was aware of the other men from the community patrol milling about on the edge of her vision, along with her daed and Mary. If she hadn't been so intent on getting answers, she would have felt intense embarrassment.

"When were you going to tell me?" Hannah asked, deciding that was the next right question that she wanted an answer to.

Abram shuffled his feet, and said," Right after I proposed to you."

Hannah knew that she had heard him correctly, but she had to ask him anyway. "When were you going to propose to me?"

"I was planning on doing it soon, but I thought it might be better as a surprise," Abram said. "But I suppose this is as good a spot as anywhere."

As his words sank into her brain, Hannah felt her heart beat faster, the sound of blood throbbing in her ears drowning out all the noise around them. He was going to ask her to marry him right now, in this moment. And then she realized that he was actually doing it. She heard him say, "I'd be honored if you'd be my wife."

"Yes," Hannah said as it echoed through her heart. "But wait. Can we really do this here? Now?"

Abram laughed. "Of course we can."

"But we're all out here trying to catch cattle thieves," Hannah groaned. "What if they came around the corner right now? They could be heavily armed. They could hurt all of us."

"We're fine," Abram said. "The thieves seem to have a pattern. None of us think that they'll try anything tonight, and if they did we are more than ready for them. This, right here, the two of us are more important than any of that."

"Then yes," Hannah said feeling her worries break away and elation rise up in her chest like she hadn't in weeks. "I would absolutely love to be your wife."

After the two of them had hugged, Hannah hurried over to her sister and her daed to tell them what had just transpired. While her daed went to talk to Abram and to shake his hand. When their daed had gone, Mary grabbed Hannah with a small squeal, and said, "So I guess he wasn't stealing our cattle, huh?"

Embarrassment raced through Hannah, but she knew that the Lord had given her all the answers she needed, and that she needed to be humble in her mistakes. "Of course not," she said. "I was wrong, but that's all part of being human. God has led us to this point, and He will continue to lead us wherever we need to go."

As she glanced over at Abram and her daed, Hannah was struck by the exact answer to her prayers, her past and her future blending seamlessly together. And she realized that by trusting the Lord, even with the uncertainties of life, she didn't have any reason to fear.

A Little Bit of Amish Faith

Alana Wilson

The streets were just beginning to get dark as Nicholas drove home. He can still hear his boss's, no, ex-boss's words echoing in the back of his mind, *I'm sorry Nicky, but we can't keep you employed if you have to call in every other day with a family emergency. It's just not how business works...* Nicholas felt himself grinding his teeth as he sped down the poorly lit backroad to his house. His headlights flashed across the wet asphalt as his mind wandered. *How am I going to tell my mom? How am I going to get groceries now and her medicine?* His mind ran circles. His headlights flashed across trees as his truck hit a patch of ice and skid. Nicholas turned the wheel hard and tried to correct the vehicle in time.

His headlights flashed across a figure that dove out of the way of his vehicle as it careened towards the ditch. Nicholas finally regained control and swerved hard. His truck skidded to a stop on the shoulder. Nicholas opened the door and slid out of the driver seat; adrenaline rushed through his body. He took shaky steps to the edge of the road. He peered down into the ditch, looking for the dark figure. They lay in the dirty snow. Nicholas slid down the bank to the figure's side. He saw in the pale twilight that it was a girl; she wore a thick dark coat over a plain dark blue dress and a starched white cap on her head. She groaned and sat up slowly.

"Are you okay?" Nicholas felt his heart pounding in his ears and his hands trembled.

"I, I think so." She replied quietly. He helped her to her feet and she groaned, leaning into him.

"I think I twisted my ankle," she said with a grimace.

"I'm so sorry. Let me take you to a doctor." Nicholas started to almost drag her up the ditch.

"Oh, no. That won't be necessary. I'm fine, really." She said shyly.

"Please let me take you to a doctor, or at least somewhere we can look at your ankle in the light." He looked at her pleadingly. He could almost see her debating it internally.

"I guess it wouldn't hurt to get it looked at, just in case it is serious," she said quietly. He sighed in relief. They scrambled up the bank to Nicholas's truck. He helped her into the passenger seat and scrambled around to his side.

"I'm so sorry, again. I didn't see you and the road was slick... I'm just so sorry." He trailed off as he looked at her face; she had a few minor scratches and scrapes.

"I forgive you. Everything happens for a reason; that is God's plan." She glanced out the window distantly.

"What are you even doing out here?" He tried to keep one eye on her and one eye on the road.

She was pretty, even in the dim light. Nicholas could see wisps of dark brown hair peeking out from under her cap and her dark green eyes were glassy. A light blush colored her cheeks. Nicolas caught a glimpse of his own nervous brown eyes in the mirror.

"I was walking back from the bakery in town. My uncle and aunt own it, and I work there whenever they need a hand. With the holidays around the corner, they're starting to get backed up with orders."

"You think they need any other help?" He chuckled nervously. She didn't respond. He drove the truck in silence. She held her hands clasped tightly in her lap.

"What's your name?" He finally said, breaking the tense silence.

"Naomi." She muttered.

"I'm Nicholas." He smiled at her.

He parked the truck outside the clinic in town. He helped Naomi out of the truck and inside. Doctor Schaffer sat at the front desk, working on paperwork; she was a middle aged woman, with streaks of gray coloring her ashy blonde hair and wrinkle just starting to appear at the corners of her eyes and mouth.

"Nicholas? Naomi? What are you two doing here so late at night? And together?" She said, and walked around the counter. Nicholas couldn't help but stare between the doctor and Naomi.

"Good evening, doctor. Nicholas here found me after I took a spill down the ditch outside town. I think I twisted my ankle." Naomi smiled sweetly up at the doctor. The doctor tutted and shook her head.

"Well, let's take you back and have a look at that ankle. Nicholas, would you mind giving me a hand here," Doctor Shaffer said, helping Naomi to her feet. Nicholas helped Naomi hobble to the exam room down the hall and onto the table.

"Well, I'll be on my way then. Will you be all right getting home, miss?" Nicholas edged towards the doorway.

"Nicolas, if you could take a seat in the waiting room, actually. I'll check on Naomi, and if it's too serious for my taste, I want you to drive her home so she doesn't overstrain herself." Doctor Shaffer smiled at Nicholas and ushered him out of the room. Nicolas wandered back to waiting room and slumped into a chair. He felt the weight of the day on his shoulders. *How could I be so stupid? I lose my job, I almost kill someone... I need to get my act together and fast,* he thought to himself. He rubbed his eyes and tried to shake the weariness.

Naomi hobbled down the hall on a crutch, back to the waiting Nicholas. He smiled shyly at her. Doctor Shaffer shuffled down the hall behind her.

"Okay, Naomi has a severe sprain and needs to stay off her ankle for a few weeks," Doctor Shaffer said, looking between the two.

"Thanks, Doc." Nicholas held open the door as Naomi hobbled outside. Nicholas helped her back into the truck. They drove down the road in silence.

"I'm sorry. Again."

"It all happened for a reason." Naomi looked out the passenger window thoughtfully.

Farms passed by as Nicholas drove down the back roads that led to the Amish community. He slowed down as the roads turned from asphalt to gravel. He stopped the truck at the gate of their community.

His headlights couldn't pierce the darkness that stretched further down the road.

"Do you need any help?" He turned to her. She looked at him, almost glared.

"No. I'll be just fine. I think you've done enough," she snarled at him and slammed the door open. She slid out of the truck and started to hobble down the dirt road. Nicholas followed her.

"Okay, I understand if you're upset. I messed up big time tonight, and you're nothing more than an innocent bystander. Please, let me try to make this right." He almost reached for her hand. Almost.

"No, this is far enough. I will be shunned by my community if they see me with you, especially in your vehicle. I can make it from here. Thank you for everything, but I hope we do not meet again in the future." She brushed an angry tear from her cheek and turned away from him.

"Let me walk with you, then. It's too dark and cold to be alone." She sighed heavily.

"Fine. But after tonight, I wish to never speak to you again," she glared at him and continued on her way.

"That's fair." Nicholas shrugged.

They walked down the dark country road in utter silence. Nicholas kept stealing glances at Naomi, trying to read her face. It occurred to him at that moment, this was the first time he had really forgotten about himself. He thought about her instead. *Is she married yet? I know the Amish girls get married young...* His thoughts wandered to who she was, what her life was like. He didn't think any more about his mother and brother waiting for him at home, or the heaviness in his heart from his father's recent passing, or the weariness in his joints from working all hours of the day.

She stopped at a tall white farm house. An old woman sat on the porch, reading by the light of a lantern. Nicholas stood at the bottom of the stairs as Naomi shuffled onto the porch. The old woman mumbled something at her. Naomi sighed and turned back to Nicholas. The old woman nodded and stood creakily.

"Nicholas, thank you for your assistance," she said quietly.

He opened his mouth to say something but she ducked inside before the words came out. Nicholas raised his hand in an awkward wave and walked back down the road. The darkness enveloped him, but for the first time in a long time, he felt clear headed. He walked in the chilly autumn night.

Nicholas sat in his truck outside his little two-story house. All the lights were off. The clock on the radio read 11:53. He trudged inside wearily. In the living room, his mother was asleep on the couch. His old lab, Gunner, greeted him at the front door with a small huff. Nicholas woke his mother up with a gentle shake.

"Mom, I'm home. Let's get to bed." He picked her up gently. She seemed to get smaller every day. He carried her down the hall and set her gently in bed. He pulled off her slippers and her fleece robe. She snuggled under the blankets with a soft sigh. He shut her door quietly behind him. Upstairs, he checked on his little brother Kevin. The fifteen-year-old boy lay deep asleep. Nicholas pulled his quilt back on him and walked down the hall to his own room. Nicholas collapsed into his bed, his shoes still on.

Nicholas woke early the next morning. His alarm blared loudly next to him. His crawled out of bed. Nicholas crept down the hall. The sun hadn't risen yet, and neither had anyone else in the house. He drove to town, trying to rub sleep from his eyes. He parked outside the diner in town and trudged inside.

He sat at the counter and drank a cup of black coffee. His phone screen glared back at him, reflecting the harsh facts of his life. *Bank account: $92.63. Mortgage due next Tuesday. Electricity bill due tomorrow.* He couldn't help but sigh heavily into his coffee. He still needed to pick up groceries and his mother's medication. As the sun finally peaked its head fully above the horizon, Nicholas walked down

Main Street. His eyes scanned the buildings looking for any 'help wanted' signs, but there were none to be seen.

But as he walked on, he did see something interesting; Naomi walking on her crutches down the other side street. Her face was red from exertion. He crossed the street at a jog and came to a stop in front of her.

"Morning," he croaked shyly.

"Hello," she growled and tried to move around him.

"Wait." He almost reached for. She stopped to listen, but didn't turn to look at him.

"I'm sorry, for last night. Do you need any help? The bakery is still a bit down the road and I'm sure it's taken you all morning to get to this point."

"And?" She snarled again.

"Let me give you a ride. Please. I want to make up for my actions," he pleaded. She was silent for a moment and then sighed.

"I guess I'm no use to my aunt if I show up at the end of the day."

"Great. Just wait here, I'll get my truck." Nicholas raced off to get his truck and pulled up next to Naomi.

They drove down the road quietly. The radio played a quiet news report, the only sound in the small cab of the truck. The bakery was just outside of town, a tourist trap. The building was squat, white-washed and impeccably clean. The parking lot was just a gravel lot. It smelled like fresh-baked bread and cinnamon rolls. He parked and helped her out of the truck.

"Well, I don't think I need any further assistance. Thank you, Nicholas." She shuffled into the bakery. Nicholas watched her go, feeling some small tug towards her. He let his feet carry his to the door and then inside. Naomi hobbled to the back on her crutches. A middle-aged woman, dressed in the same clothes as Naomi came out.

"Good morning, how can I help you?" She smiled politely at Nicholas.

"Oh, I was wondering if I could help you actually. I'm an acquaintance of Naomi's and I know she has a pretty bad sprain, so I was hoping I could help out until she's feeling better." He felt his cheeks burn. The woman studied him for a minute. She raised a finger to him and the disappeared into the back. He could hear the hushed voices as Naomi and the woman talked. The woman came back and looked Nicholas up and down.

"If you'd like to help, you are to be here from dawn to dusk. What is your work ethic like?"

"I'm willing to do anything. I can lift things and I'm good with tools and I can be here early or late or whatever you need." His heart raced. Naomi glared at him from the doorway.

"Alright then. You'll be paid every week, in cash of course. How does $300 a week sound? And this will be temporary, just until Naomi is back on her feet." The woman laughed now. Nicholas smiled.

"This is great. I can start right now. If you need me to." He felt giddy now.

"Ay, get back there and start moving those flour sacks from the back door to the pantry." He slid past the woman and almost tripped over Naomi's crutch.

Nicholas was satisfied in this new work. It was labor-intensive, which he didn't mind. But what he liked the most was picking up Naomi in the mornings. She had gotten permission from her community for Nicholas to pick her up at the gates and to drive her to work. They would talk sometimes early in the morning, about their favorite books, the weather, their families. He learned so much about her; she lived with her aunt and uncle, who owned the bakery she worked at, and her grandmother lived with them. She shared a room with her six cousins; four boys and two girls. She learned that he lived with his mother and younger brother. He had worked many job since dropping out of high school to take care of sick mother. He had played a game called lacrosse in school and he tried to explain the game to her on multiple occasions.

When they worked together, Nicholas couldn't help but look at Naomi from time to time. Her aunt had set up a stool at the front counter so she wouldn't have to stand all day. He would sometimes stare, and then catch himself and get back to work. He would chastise himself every time. But he couldn't help but notice how pretty she would look, like when she had smidges of flour smeared on her face or the smile she would use when her uncle told a joke while they sat in the kitchen baking loaf after loaf of bread. But she looked the nicest when they sat in his truck after work, when the sun came in the passenger window just right and caught a few stray hairs that had slipped out from under her cap during the day and made her cheeks look rosy and full. One day, after Nicholas had worked been driving her for a few weeks, Naomi looked at him curiously.

"I understand that you live with your mother and brother, but would you mind if I asked what happened to your father?"

"He didn't run off if that's what you're asking," Nicholas chuckled," He was, uh, killed a few months ago in a drunk driving accident. It's been rough on my mom and Kevin, but it's been getting better."

"I'm sorry to hear that. My parents passed when I was quite young. Also from an auto accident." She looked down at her hands soberly.

"That sucks. I'm sorry that happened to you. Doesn't God just have a sick sense of humor?" Nicholas wanted to punch himself in the face for opening his stupid mouth.

"God doesn't have a sense of humor. Everything He plans, it is for a reason." She replied calmly.

"Oh really? So God killed my dad and made my mother sick for some important reason," Nicholas snarled at her.

"Yes. What is your mother sick with?" She studied Nicholas's face.

"Cancer. It's terminal."

"I'm sorry. But did you think ever think God gives His hardest battles to His most worthy children?" She smiled at him.

"Why?" Nicholas stared straight ahead at the road.

"Because there will always be evil in the world and God must make sure He has soldiers to fight that evil, on earth and from heaven," she said, getting a powerful air behind her voice. Something intense, passionate.

"So, my mom and dad are soldiers for God?" Nicholas scoffed lightly.

"Most likely. If not, then they have a good place in heaven for them, something peaceful and rewarding." She smiled peacefully, as if thinking about what Heaven looks like.

"That's, that's actually really nice to think about. Thank you, Naomi." He noticed from the corner of his eye the small blush creeping up her neck.

Weeks passed and autumn turned into winter. Nicholas became a fixture at the bakery at the edge of town; something was always needing to be fixed and Naomi's cousins were a bit too young to be working there yet. He fixed ceiling tiles and the siding outside. He helped Naomi's uncle repair the window panes and learned how to make everything from a loaf of bread to the biggest wedding cake with pristine white frosting. He discovered he had a knack for frosting cupcakes and kneading dough. He continued to drive Naomi to the bakery and couldn't wait to see her every morning.

"Nicholas, I got you a present," she said one day, sliding a brown paper package across the seat to Nicholas as he picked her up one morning. He raised an eyebrow and opened the present. Inside, a long navy scarf sat folded neatly. He pulled it on and almost blushed; it smelled like Naomi.

"Thank you, this is wonderful Naomi." The thick scarf was warm and soft on his neck.

"Oh, I just thought you could use something warm, since it's cold out and you don't really wear anything besides that jacket," she trailed off as her red nose was matched with a red blush. He reached over and took her hand, looking her in the eye.

"Seriously, thank you, Naomi." She blushed harder and looked away. Nicholas still caught the little smile that stayed on her face for the rest of the day.

Nicholas looked through the window at the jewelry sitting on the velvet display. Everything was going good; the bills were all paid, he had presents for his mother and brother for Christmas. But something was missing. Silver watches and gold chains sat on the black cloth, glittering at him. *I can't afford any of these thing... She probably wouldn't even like it...* He had never seen Naomi wear anything other than her plain dresses and stark white cap. She wore thick gloves and a heavy coat now that it was winter, but she didn't wear makeup or jewelry. He wracked his brain trying to think of something she would actually like.

He walked down the street. It was Sunday night, the only day he got off from the bakery. They were going to close a few days before Christmas and a few days after to celebrate with their community, so Nicholas wanted to get something for Naomi before the holiday. His thoughts wandered as the snow began to fall in thick flakes. He wasn't paying attention and bumped into a girl walking the opposite direction; he knocked the bags from her hands.

"Oh, jeez. I'm so sorry. I didn't mean to." He started to pick up her bags.

"You said that when we first met." She said. Nicholas looked up at her and froze. Naomi stood there, wearing her hair down in soft curls and a cute sweater dress. She wore some makeup, just enough to highlight but not overpower.

"Naomi," he muttered.

"Surprise," she said softly.

"What are you doing here? Don't you need to," he trailed off as he took her in completely.

"I just needed to come into town, and it feels better to look like an English, to blend in better. I saw you from across the street and thought I might surprise you." She smiled and took her bags from him.

"This is a surprise. I was just doing some shopping myself." He blushed slightly.

"Well, then would you mind escorting me home. I like to walk on nights like this when the air is crisp and you can see the stars so clearly." She took his arm and they walked down the street.

They walked quietly for a long time. She grasped his hand firmly; her cold fingers felt so tiny in his. He held her bags in his other hand, like a gentleman. Their breaths billowed in tiny clouds. Cars didn't pass by them in the quiet night. The only sound was their feet crunching through the snow.

"So what did you need to buy," he joked.

"Just a few things from the hardware store. My uncle ran out of nails and he wants to finish up some presents for my cousins so I ran out to get some."

"You're so sweet," he chuckled and squeezed her hand gently.

"So what were you doing in town so late," she teased back.

"Just looking for a present," he shrugged. "For my mom," he added quickly.

"That's very sweet of you, Nicholas. So what were you thinking of getting her?"

"Oh, I can't decide. I wanted to get something nice and fancy for her, but also something practical like a sweater. She does like sweaters. Or a new pair of slippers, ones with thick lining." He had already bought her a thick sweater and a pair of slippers that looked like cats, because she liked silly things like that.

"How about some thick socks?" Nicholas laughed hard at her. "Oh, I know, socks! How exciting! But she's sick, so some thick socks would be nice in case her toes are cold," she chuckled softly.

"That's a really good idea, actually. Thank you." He wanted to kiss her. But he didn't. They were friends, co-workers. He didn't want to impose on her beliefs either. He knew that the Amish were conservative and he didn't want to make her uncomfortable. They stopped outside the gates.

"I'll see you tomorrow." She looked up at him, and he swore she batted her eyelashes at him.

"Yeah. Tomorrow. Good night, Naomi." He smiled back as her fingers slipped from his and she took her bag back.

"Good night, Nicholas." She waved at him and walked down the lane.

Nicholas woke early the next morning. His present for Naomi sat on his desk. He grabbed his jacket and crept down the hall, the present tucked under his arm. He snuck to his mother's door and peaked in. She lay there, sleeping peacefully, a small smile on her face. He crossed the room to wake her up. He shook her arm gently. She was cold. He crossed the room and left. On the front porch, he pulled out his phone.

"Hello? Hi, yes, I need an ambulance. I think my mom is dead," he said blankly.

Nicholas sat on the front porch with Kevin. The flashing lights were blindingly bright. An officer squeezed Nicholas's shoulder and gave him a pitiful look. Kevin looked blankly ahead with red rimmed eyes. The paramedic walked down the stairs and stood in front of the boys. She smiled weakly at them.

"I'm sorry boys. Your mom was a good lady. I hear she was a great teacher. She passed in her sleep, so it was painless. She's in a better place now." Nicholas wanted to believe her but he just felt so angry.

After everyone left, it was deathly quiet. Nicholas called into the high school so Kevin wouldn't have to go in. Kevin sat on the couch, wrapped in their mother's favorite blanket. Nicholas didn't know what to say to him. He didn't have any words. *What kind of God orphans a boy?* Nicholas walked down the road aimlessly.

He found himself en route to the bakery and couldn't stop himself. *They would want to know why he was late.* He walked into the warm bakery and saw Naomi's aunt at the counter.

"Nicholas? Are you all right?" She walked around the counter nervously.

"Yeah, I'm fine. My mom died last night," he croaked.

"Oh Nicholas." She hugged him gently. Tears welled in his eyes. Naomi came from the back at that moment.

"Nicholas?" She wiped her hands on rag. He sniffled and left quickly. Outside, in the cold air, tears burned down his face. He heard the down shut behind him and someone grab his hand. He sniffled and wiped the tears roughly from his face.

"Nicholas? I thought you were hurt when you didn't show up this morning." Naomi sounded worried.

"I'm okay. My mom died last night. "He shivered from the cold. He turned to look at her.

"I'm so sorry, Nicholas," she said softly. He took her hands gently.

"Why? Why did she have to die?" He sobbed. Naomi hugged him tightly.

"It's God's will. She's in a better place." She muttered against his coat.

"But why? It's cruel! My brother is orphaned now! We're all alone now. Why would God do that to us?" He cried into her shoulder. She was much shorter than him, but he still held her tightly.

"I don't know, Nicholas. I'm sorry, but I don't have all the answers. Maybe He didn't want her to suffer any longer. And your brother has you. You have each other. You can always build a bigger family." She shushed him and rubbed his back soothingly.

"I don't know what to do any more, Naomi." He rubbed away the tears again.

"Just make it through today. Then make it through tomorrow. And that you aren't alone in this. You have people who will help you." She smiled sweetly up at him. He managed a weak smile back.

"Thank you." He said softly.

"Nicholas, I'm going to go back inside now. It's freezing out here!" She giggled and led him back inside the bakery.

Nicholas sat in the bakery that day, just watching. Naomi's aunt wouldn't let him work, so instead she made him drink hot tea and taste-test pastries. He felt empty inside. But he felt better knowing that Naomi was his friend, at least. She kept glancing at him throughout the day; when she caught his she offered only a smile.

"Nicholas, would you like to walk home with me?" Naomi pulled on her coat tightly as the sun dipped below the horizon.

"Oh, sure." He followed her out the door quietly.

The streets of the town were lit with bright Christmas lights. Nicholas felt tired. He hadn't felt this tired since he had first met Naomi. She took his hand as they walked. He shoved his hand in his other pocket, and felt her present, long forgotten from this morning. He blushed, thinking about how much he had wanted to give it to her in his truck this morning.

"Naomi, I know this is a bad time, but I got you a present. I know I'm not going to see you for like a week, so I wanted to get you something before the holiday. I was going to give it to you this morning but you know..." he trailed off. He took the present out and handed it to Naomi. She smiled up at him.

"Thank you, Nicholas. I know this must be hard." She ripped off the bright red wrapping paper and shoved it in her pocket. She opened the box carefully. Inside, nestled in white tissue paper was a book. It was an old Nancy Drew book of his mother's. He had asked her last night when he got home if he could give it to Naomi.

"I know you said you hadn't read anything good in a long time and my mom had this one lying around. I figured you might like something to read over the holiday and just enjoy." He blushed fiercely under the streetlights.

"Oh, Nicholas. That's so thoughtful. Thank you." She said and kissed his cheek gently. She stowed the book in her own pocket and they walked on. Her fingers laced through his. He felt his heart beating against his rib cage. At the edge of the Amish community, Naomi looked up at him. The night was quiet, peaceful.

"Nicholas, what are we doing," she whispered.

"I don't know. But it's working, isn't it?" He looked deep into her eyes.

"Is it? To be friends is one thing, but to be something more."

"Naomi, let's talk about this later, okay? Let's just be with our families now," he said back tensely.

"You're right. I'm sorry. Go and be with your brother. If you need anything, let me know. Please." She squeezed his hand and turned away from him.

"Thank you, Naomi. For everything," he called to her as she walked down the lane. She looked back over her shoulder and smiled sweetly at him.

At home, Nicholas found his brother asleep on the couch. He slumped against the doorway and rubbed his face. Christmas was just around the corner and it was going to be lonely. Their mother had been the one who set up the Christmas tree and always made them a big breakfast on Christmas morning. He couldn't imagine how empty the couch was going to look on Christmas morning, without their mother sitting there. He woke Kevin up and ushered him to bed. Nicholas collapsed into his own bed, wishing someone were there to hold him. Someone small, with wavy chocolate brown and deep green eyes.

Christmas morning was bleak. Kevin sat glaring at the stack of presents that were for their mother. Nicholas couldn't bear to open the present from his mother. Kevin locked himself in his room. Nicholas opened his mother's presents and cried. Kevin had gotten her a new travel book, for Mongolia. Nicholas stared blankly at the cozy slippers he had bought. Nicholas sat on the porch and read that travel book. He wished he was far away too. He wished he was happy again, wished his brother could be happy again. He wished Naomi was by his side. He wished he had her faith and grace. He looked up as Kevin sat down next to him.

"Hey, Nick."

"How you holding up, buddy?" He closed the book absentmindedly.

"I'm..." He shrugged.

"I'm sorry we can't have a big Christmas dinner or something. Something to make it all..." Nicholas couldn't find the words.

"It's fine. I understand, dude." They sat in silence for a while. The sun began to dip and the snow began falling. Kevin finally stood and went inside. Nicholas sighed. He stood to go inside when he heard someone coming up the gravel driveway. Naomi stood at the bottom of his stairs, holding a basket. She wore her English sweater dress and leggings. A knit hat kept her wavy hair in check.

"Merry Christmas, Nicholas." She said softly.

"Merry Christmas, Naomi. What are you doing here?" Nicholas helped her up the stairs.

"Helping the less fortunate," she teased," Are you going to invite me in? I've got a big dinner that I need to get started."

"Of course, come in." Nicholas was dazed. He took her coat and led her into the kitchen. She smiled sweetly at him as she started cooking. Kevin glanced at him from the stairs.

"You want to come down and meet Naomi? She knows I can't cook and came to make sure you didn't die of starvation," he joked. Kevin shrugged and shuffled down the stairs. Nicholas led him into the kitchen.

"Naomi? Sorry to interrupt, but this is my brother, Kevin. Kevin, this is my friend, Naomi." Naomi smiled and offered her hand. Kevin shook it weakly. Kevin turned to Nicholas.

"She's pretty," he remarked and trudged into living room.

"He seems to be doing okay." She turned back to the cutting board.

"Yeah. He's just jealous he can't snag a nice girl like you," he flirted and then blushed heavily. Naomi blushed slightly too.

"So, how have you been?" She didn't look up from the vegetables she was cutting.

"It's been rough. It's nice to see you, though. I've kind of missed seeing you every day." He pulled a soda out of the fridge and hopped up onto the counter next to her.

"I've missed talking to you, too, Nicholas. It's been quiet. Food will be done in about forty-five minutes." She smiled at him, and Nicholas swore his heart skipped a beat. She looked so natural in his kitchen.

"I finished that book you gave me. And the note inside was sweet." She glanced at him.

"Note?" He raised an eyebrow.

"From your mother? She just said that she was glad I was your friend and that she couldn't be more thankful that somebody had gotten you out of your shell."

"Oh, I didn't know she wrote that. That's so like her." He muttered. He couldn't help but smile at the thought of his mother always looking out for him.

"She must've been quite a woman to have raised you and your brother."

"She was. I miss her." He sipped his soda pensively. Naomi placed her hand on his knee gently. He grasped it and gave her fingers a gentle squeeze.

"Why don't you set the table? It'll only take a few more moments." She smiled gently at him.

They sat around the dinner table. The silence was almost palpable. Kevin poked at the carrots and potatoes on his plate. Nicholas kept stealing glances at Naomi. Naomi didn't take her eyes off her plate either. Nicholas cleared his throat loudly.

"Kevin, what do you think?" Nicholas fixed his younger brother with a hard stare.

"It's good. Thank you, Naomi." He mumbled into his roast potatoes. Nicholas kicked him under the table.

"So, what are you learning in school, Kevin? I didn't get to go to high school," Naomi asked.

"Evolution." Kevin snarled. He stood and left the table.

"Kevin!" Nicholas stood and shouted at him.

"It's okay, Nicholas. He's just feeling hurt. Let him be, he'll come around." Naomi squeezed his hand. Nicholas sat slowly and looked at her. His heart sped up as she battered her lashes slowly at him.

"What are you saying, Naomi?" He felt her small hand in his; it felt like it was two halves made whole.

"Well, if you'll have me, I'd like to stay." She stared at his hands.

"On one condition," he whispered.

"Yes?" She looked deep into his eyes. He could stare at her eyes for forever.

"Kiss me. Please." She smiled and leaned forward slightly. He closed the gap between them and pressed his lips against hers. Time seemed to stop in that second; he was aware of only her in the room. He kept his hands firmly on the table, afraid of startling her like a deer. She leaned back slowly.

"I should go talk to Kevin," Nicholas breathed. His heart still pounded against his chest.

"I'll be right here," she giggled. And unspoken, *I'll be waiting*, hung between them.

Nicholas climbed the stairs and almost ran down the hall to Kevin's room. He knocked loudly. No response. He cracked the door to find Kevin sitting on his bed. Kevin didn't look at him.

"Hey buddy."

"So, your girlfriend is going to be my new mom?" Kevin said blankly. Nicholas sat on the edge of Kevin's bed and sighed.

"No, not at all. She's just here because, I guess, she loves me. She knows what it's like to lose her parents. She's not going to be your new mom or anything more than my girlfriend. But she's going to have a rough time adjusting to this role."

"What?" Kevin looked at Nicholas like Nicholas had grown a second head.

"She's Amish. She's not quite up to date with all the relationship standards of us regular people," he chuckled.

"So?"

"So just come downstairs and give her a chance. Eat something besides a pop tart or ramen. I mean, she did cook us actual food."

"Okay, but just dinner. I'm not sticking around for dessert." Kevin trudged to the door and down the stairs.

As they sat around the table again, Nicholas felt a weight fall off his shoulders, a weight he forgot he was carrying. Nicholas saw his future at that dinner table, and he liked what he saw. He was at peace, at last.

AMISH GUILT

MAYA MILLER

Her mother had always told Rachel, "Darling, divorce is for the weak that do not honor the decisions of our maker," whenever they heard community news or gossip about a broken marriage or divorce. It was just not something that her mother believed should be done – under any circumstances.

And Rachel lived to please others. It was just the way that God had made *her*. She did not want to let her mother down. She did not want to let her community down. She did not believe for a minute that women that chose divorce were weak or sinful, but she feared the pain of being judged as weak. She feared the disappointment that she would incite in her family, especially her mother, if that would ever be something that she would need to consider.

So that was why when her oldest friend in the world, Samuel, encouraged her to sneak away in the night and start a new life, she stubbornly refused. That was why, each and every time she felt the same sickening, sharp, agonizing blows reverberate through her entire physical being, she simply clenched her teeth and prayed for it to be over. And that was why she learned to keep her posture demure even through the pain; her dress and hair completely neat, perfect ad covering her skin; and her flinching at gentle contact by others to a minimum. Others saw a flawless, happy young bride on the verge of entering motherhood with an attentive ad protective husband. Younger girls envied her ability to always carry and dress herself just so, even when they should not have allowed themselves to envy. But what the community did not know, and what they could not see, was that the perfection and poise that she demonstrated to the world was merely the only lifeline she had in an otherwise tumultuous and hopeless reality.

Market day was always Rachel's most and least favorite day. It was her most favorite because she loved having an excuse to leave the house and go out into the community unaccompanied by Walter, or her parents. It was perfectly acceptable in their society for her to do so anytime that she wanted, but her husband did not allow it, with the exception of market day. She was allowed a "stipend," Walter called it, to purchase only necessities for their home and health. "Anything beyond that, you will ask me, and I will give you my answer as to whether I think you need and deserve an item," he had announced on the day after their wedding. He had given her quite a number of instructions that day, in fact. She could not leave the house alone without him or his or her parents; she could not speak with other men within ten years of their age unless he was with her; she was to keep the house clean; she was to only prepare certain meals that he would decree; she was to keep herself presentable; and she was not to argue with him. He continued on from there, with further instructions, and then ended with a level stare into her eyes, stating "and I will punish your insubordination in any way that I see fit. You have been provided by God for me to have dominion over, and I will use that power for whatever I see fit." She had stood on in appalled silence, disguised as obedience, devastated by the fact that she was now tied for her entire life to a cruel, monstrous man.

For the first four months of their marriage, Rachel did her very best to follow the rules and demands of her husband. Inside her head she leveled him with insults and made refusals, stating things like "I am a person and deserve the right to have a rest or enjoy my days" inside her head. But she never uttered such things aloud. In fact, she was productive, obedient and attractive. She lived-up to all the standards in place in the community and more. Her skills were noticed and adopted by others. Her general appearance made those around her smile. Community members assumed that she stayed so much in the house to simply show her husband how much she loved him through her work. He had his way with her ever night, and she was dreading the day that she would realize that she was with child. And through it all, she begged people with her eyes to help her. Sadly no one saw or heard the agony that she was living in.

And then one day it started. She had not seen it coming. She thought that he had already done his worst, denying food or money if she made a mistake. But once the back of Walter's hand made contact with her soft, white cheek, she saw that there was so much more suffering in store for her.

That first backhand slap across the face actually turned out to be a rare even, however. Usually he would save the hits and grips that caused bruises for the parts of her body that would be hidden under the generous clothing that the women of the community wore. It made it easier for him, in his depravity, because the only parts of her body that he really need worry about were her face and upper neck and her hands. Other than there, he had given himself free license over her body, physically and sexually.

Her oldest friend, Samuel, suspected that something was wrong, but she would never confirm it, and warned him to keep quiet about ungrounded suspicions. That particular market day, she was at his family's table at the market, picking out the kinds of vegetables that she by now knew her husband would want. She saw a beautiful squash there that made her mouth water, and placed it in her basket on the ground next to her. But after she thought about it, she realized that purchasing it would mean angering Walter who hated squash. She turned to fetch it from her basket and caught her breath as a shooting pain lanced through her back from the previous night's injuries.

"Rach, what's wrong with your back?" he said as she straightened, more stiffly than she would have liked.

"Oh, nothing. I'm fine," she said as cheerily as she could muster. "I just twisted at a funny angle when I bent down."

Samuel simply stared at her long enough that it became uncomfortable in its obviousness, and Rachel became nervous because she knew from past experience that Walter had spies that would tell him if she was spending too long speaking with any man in particular. He had a huge dislike for Samuel because of their close friendship and had done everything that he could, short of forbidding her to speak to him, to stop that friendship. Samuel was from a well-connected community family, and Walter never picked on the strong, only the weak. The irony of this fact was never lost on Rachel, who had grown-up with that idea that women who left bad marriages were weak – and those that stayed were strong. That should have meant that Walter would not dare pick on her in all of her strength, but obviously there was a disconnect somewhere. Maybe she did not yet know what true strength was, or maybe he was not smart enough to.

"You can't lie to me, Rach. You've never been able to."

She kept that fake public smile plastered to her face and feigned confusion. "I'm not lying, Sammy. I don't have anything to lie about."

"Remember when you stole my jacks on our first day of school?" He retorted with the smallest of half grins.

That brought a genuine smile to her face. "I didn't steal them. You gave them to me," she said in the rehearsed way she always did to keep their old joke going.

"Okay, now that we've established that I won't put up with any lies, can you please tell me what is wrong with your back? Did he do it again?" There was fire in Samuel's eyes now. He had always hated Walter and absolutely loathed him now that he knew that he was rough with Rachel. The reality was that he would likely find a way to kill Walter if he really knew what he did to her, but she had never shared the extent of the behavior. She did not want her friend to be arrested for murder. But Walter dying, that would actually be pretty great.

She felt her cheeks get hot under her best friend's scrutiny. "Sammy, please," she whispered, not really knowing what she was asking him for. She took a step closer and lowered her voice to a quiet whisper. "I don't know how to stop it." The tears that burned the back of her eyes would betray her to anyone watching this conversation, but she was dangerously close to the point where she could no longer blink them back.

Samuel leaned in further – not enough to make the conversation look intimate, but enough so that a passerby at the market would not hear what he was about to say. His eyes softened. "Just leave him. Ask the community for help. Ask *me* for help, Rachel."

"You know I can't just leave him. You know why I can't seek out a divorce."

"Rach, your reasons for not being able to leave him seem pretty weak in the face of the pain that he is causing you. You need to find a way to walk away. I need you to find a way to let yourself get out. Find peace with divorce. Find it in yourself to change your heart about this. I will protect you. I need my best friend alive and kicking, or what have I got? You can use your new heart to make a new start. I can help you."

"It's just not that easy, Sammy. I can't let everyone down. I can't be that person." Her shoulders sagged under the renewed understanding of the situation that she was in. No matter what happened, she would be letting down someone she loved. Her best friend hoped against hope that she would leave, and the rest of the community put faith in what an amazing existence she led and would not understand her walking away.

Samuel straightened up and the anger that was there before flashed anew. "That's not enough of a reason anymore, Rachel. He's hurting you. I know he is, even though you won't show me the bruises he leaves hidden like you on a coward."

"What are you two talking about so privately over here?" The jovial voice of Samuel's father boomed loudly in Rachel's ears and across the market.

Instinctively both she and Samuel took a step back and straightened. "Hi Pa, did you bring the rest of the squash and tomatoes?"

And just like that the conversation was over, at least in that moment. "Well, Sammy, thank you for the beautiful vegetables and I will see you next week." She plastered on her public smile and gave a wave as she turned away, purposefully not looking at his face as she left. To everyone around her it would it would never seem as if Samuel had not just been asking her to make the most difficult decision she had ever had to face. And that is what she needed it to look like until she could figure out what to do.

She always took her time walking home from the market on these days, no matter the weather. Today was a particularly lovely day and she took advantage. She felt like a prisoner that was let out once a week, and she took full advantage of the freedom. She was cognizant of the fact that too much sun could burn her skin, however, and she did not linger too long, as she knew that Walter wanted her skin "white and milky, as a woman should be."

She hated that she was married to a person that would think such a thing. She hated that she was stuck with a husband that was not really a man. And that was just the truth. A real man would not treat a woman the way that her husband did. And Samuel was right, he was a coward, but it was even worse than that. He purposefully guided his attacks to hit the parts of her body that would be hidden. It was not young passion in the heat of an angry moment. It was sustained. It was pre-meditated. It was evil.

The cold fear that gripped her as she stepped across the threshold into what should have been her happy marital home was always stifling, particularly because each market day she would make the active decision to return to a situation that she knew could not last. The fear of divorce and letting everyone down paralyzed her, and was compounded by the reality that she truly tried to hide from herself – she was absolutely terrified of her husband.

Her eyes adjusting from the bright sunny day to dark interior of her entryway hid from immediate view the hand that shot out and grabbed her by the shoulder of her dress and dragged her body completely into shadow before the front door slammed and clicked. Unfortunately, the temporarily blindness did nothing to cushion the blow as her husband's knuckles struck her left cheek, sending her spinning and hitting the inside of the doorway with her right cheek . She saw lights and felt pain, unlike anything that she had ever felt, even at his hand. Pain and shock silenced any instinctive cry that should have come.

"You continue to bring this on yourself, my darling." His voice was cold and quiet.

She reached out to steady herself on the wall and the side of her face that had just hit the wall suddenly took another blow from his knuckles, harder than the fist, sending her body plummeting to the ground. She had enough time to wonder what in the world she could have done to bring on such a violent attack when the blows started coming again. She could not focus on anything with her eyes as his fists and feet made contact after contact, blow after blow. The sickening sound of solid parts of his body, slamming into the delicate skin and flesh of her body sounded in an almost continuous refrain, as he unleashed unimaginable brutality on her. Maybe she cried out and maybe not. She couldn't be sure, as he never allowed her a moment to get her bearings or catch her breath. At some point the torment became incessant and she no longer felt each individual blow. Vaguely she realized that there was a crack and then another, but by that point, she didn't feel the cause distinctly.

After a time, she did not know if it was long or short, she became aware that the actual new hits had stopped. She twisted her head to look up, not having the strength to lift her head. The light coming through the window behind his head put Walter in silhouette, but she could tell that he used a cloth to wipe his hands as he stared down at her. "You are such a disappointment as a wife, Rachel," he said calmly. "Did you really think that I wouldn't know that you traipse off every week to see Samuel at the market like a common whore?" He crouched down and tilted his head as he looked at her. "Now your face is ugly enough to match who you are." He spit on the rag that he was using to wipe his hands and reached out to roughly smear it across her cheek. You have some blood on your face. Get cleaned up before I come home for dinner." And with that he stood and casually excited the house, closing the front door behind him.

As soon as the door clicked, Rachel's tears started. The pain was insurmountable. She couldn't move and when she tried, sharp pain shot through her ribs. She knew that her face was swelling up because it started getting harder to blink. She gave up on her attempts to stand and simply rested her head on the ground, wondering distantly if he would kill her when he came home to an empty kitchen, before she passed out completely.

Rachel was woken sometime later by a knocking on the door. As she came to, pain lanced through so many parts of her body at once that she could not even distinguish them all. She did her best to breathe through her nose to prevent the vomit that was pushing at the back of her throat from coming up. The disorientation was profound, as her muddled mind struggled to figure out where she was and why she hurt so badly. It all came back to her in a rush of confusion and terror. Walter had almost killed her. She did not know how long she had been there on the floor, but there was still light coming through the windows, which was good. Walter never returned home before the sun had set.

The knocking got louder and a deep voice called out, "Mrs. Webber, are you there?"

She did not have the strength to answer or move, and hoped that whoever that was would come in and help her up, or she would likely die where she lay.

The door opened slowly and stopped against the bag of food from the market that lay discarded on the floor next to her. "Mrs. Webber? It's Amos Bayler, your neighbor."

She tried to speak but it came out as a choked cry. It was loud enough though, that he obviously heard it, because his head peaked around the door. As soon as he saw her his eyes widened and he rushed over to her, lowering himself to his knees next to her twisted form.

"Mrs. Webber, my God." He gently, but firmly untwisted her limbs and helped her lay more comfortably, if there was such a thing when a body was as broken as hers. "I need to leave you for a moment to get some help," he said, starting to stand.

"Please, wait," she croaked out with intense effort. He lowered himself back down and leaned in to hear her better. "Not my husband."

He opened his mouth, likely to ask why. But then his eyes first widened in understanding and then narrowed in anger. With a curt nod, he stood and said in a gentle voice, not matching the ferocity on his face, "I will be back in a minute."

Rachel didn't know why, but despite the pain and vulnerability of that moment, she felt safe having Amos Bayler there. She let herself succumb and the world around her went black.

* * *

When Rachel came to, she was in a strange place. The air was cold, but her body was under warm blankets. There were beeping sounds and a whooshing sound that she recognized as an air conditioner from the times that she had been in other office buildings or stores. Still disoriented, she tried to sit up and groaned. Her entire body hurt and she realized there were ropes attached to her body, pulling on her hands and nose. Suddenly panicked, she pushed herself up through the pain and started to pull at the ropes.

"Rachel, wait." A man's deep voice froze her efforts. She knew it wasn't Walter's voice because even though it was deep, it was gentle.

Walter always spoke with a harsh scowl on his face when he addressed her. There was never any of the compassion and concern that she heard in this person's voice. Looking up, she realized that the voice belonged to the handsome neighbor that she had never dared speak to in fear of retribution from her husband.

"Amos Bayler. What are you doing here? What are these ropes?"

"Rachel, you're at the hospital. Do you remember at all what happened to you today?" He took a few tentative steps forward as he spoke.

Suddenly a woman in bright purple scrubs, whom she didn't recognize, entered the room with a clipboard and started reading the beeping machines and taking down notes. She began fiddling with the ropes, which Rachel now recognized as being IV lines. "Hello, honey. How are you feeling?" She busied herself with more notes and charts.

"I hurt a lot."

The woman's eyes were kind. "I know you do, sweetie. Just lay back and rest. Here, let me adjust the bed a bit for you." Once she was sure that Rachel was comfortable, she said "I'll be back in a few minutes with something for the pain and I think that the hospital social worker is going to want to speak with you when you feel a bit stronger. "

"Okay, thank you," Rachel said, overwhelmed by waking up in such a foreign place.

"Amos, I don't recognize that nurse. What hospital is this?"

"I brought you to Central." He held his hands up like he was worried that she would be angry, and he was surrendering.

"Central?" She was shocked.

"Why would you go to so much trouble? What happened to me? You've never even spoken to me. My husband is not kind to you." She felt a warm rush of gratitude, eclipsed by that still lingering confusion.

"I just...well, I saw you there on the floor and...do you remember what happened?" He sat down in the chair next to her hospital bed.

He obviously was struggling with what to say to her, and she wanted to know why.

"I remember Walter being angry. I remember...well, he lost his temper like I've never seen him do before." Amos' eyes were hard and he nodded, but did not comment. "Then I remember...you. You, like an angel to save me. And then everything went black."

"I was coming over to borrow a tool. I had seen your husband leave and hadn't had time to catch him. But I figured that you would be able to give it to me. I was working on something for the elders and they suggested I borrow it. And that's when I found you there on the ground."

"I'm sorry," she said, suddenly overwhelmed with the understanding of what that must have been like for him.

He closed his eyes and took a deep breath. When he opened them again, his eyes were nearly black. "Please do not ever again apologize to me for what your gutless husband has done to you. He deserves more than what will come to him. And that I know to be true."

Amos was angry. Rachel could tell that, but for some reason it did not scare her the way that it did when Walter was angry. "I can trust you," she simply stated.

"Yes, you can," was his simple reply.

They sat in silence for a few minutes. She closed her eyes and rested against the pillows, taking stock of what hurt in her body. Her ribs on her left side were throbbing and it hurt all over her torso to take a deep breath. Her limbs felt like they had been seen a fall of a cliff or a buggy accident. And her face stung and throbbed at the same time. She couldn't see clearly out of her left eye. She wondered if there was any internal damage. Flashes of memory from the beating started to cross her mind. She had never thought him capable of losing control the way that he had. He was always so controlled in his abuse, so deliberate. This had been passionate, evil in a different way. He wanted to kill her. What could have possibly have provoked such a reaction? And then, suddenly, she remembered. Samuel. Walter had called her a whore for speaking to her friend. And suddenly it was too much, and she cried. She cried, and then sobbed for what seemed like forever. Amos put his hand out for her to hold, and it became her lifeline. She gasped for air through her tears, as shooting pain jabbed at her ribs.

They sat like that for a long time, even after her tears had subsided. She half expected Walter to come crashing through the door demanding to know why she was holding this man's hand, but strangely enough, that did not scare her as much as it probably should have. Amos made her feel safe and cared for, something that her husband had never done for her.

"Amos," she said after a long stretch of silence.

"Yes?"

"Why did you take me to Central instead of the village hospital?" She had never had anyone go out of their way like that, and she was still having trouble comprehending why. She was always the one that went above and beyond for other people, not the other way around.

"I just wanted to give you some privacy. There are going to be questions about where you've gone, but there would be so many more about what had happened to you if you were in the village hospital. As you heard, they are obligated to get the social workers and possibly police involved, so that would mean that the entire village would know what was happening to you. It is nothing to be ashamed of, at least for you. Walter should be very ashamed. But I wanted to give you the chance to figure out how you want to approach this with your family and the community." He paused, and added in a slightly less gentle tone, "And I know that you care so much about the community and what they think."

Without knowing why, the last part of his statement bothered Rachel. "Why do you say I care about the community and what it thinks like it's is a bad thing?"

"Oh, Rachel, it's not a bad thing most of the time. But you do it at the expense of your own health and safety. You have been putting on a pretense, I suspect since your marriage started, that all is well and you are the perfect wife and community member. What has he been doing, hiding his abuse purposefully? Has he been intentionally hurting you under where your dress would sit? That is insane." His voice got more and more forceful as he ranted. And by the end he was standing, breathing heavily and running his hands through his hair.

Suddenly feeling a twinge of fear, Rachel said, "Amos, please calm down. You're scaring me."

His eyes went wide and he immediately sat down again, an apology written all over his face. "Oh, Rachel, I'm such a fool. I'm so sorry. If you would like me to leave, please just tell me."

"No," she practically shouted at him. "Please don't leave, unless you want to."

"I don't want to. I'll stay with you until it's time to go home, if that is what you need. No one should ever be alone, and I will make sure that you stay safe."

What he did not say was that he would keep her safe from Walter, should be bother to show his face at the hospital. Although, he was a complete coward, and leaving the community would mean that he would be unprotected, and he would never allow that to happen when all of his power was from preying on the weak.

There was a knock on the door and a small blond woman in a streamlined navy dress click-clacked her heels into the room. "Mrs. Webber?" Her voice was all business, but not unkind.

"Yes." She hated the last name. It made the hair on the back of her neck stand on end.

"My name is Shelia Winter. I am a social worker here at Central Hospital. I work specifically with women and children that come to the hospital with injuries consistent with physical abuse." She looked at Amos with loathing on her face. "Are *you* Mr. Webber?"

"No I'm not. If I was, you would never be needed for this woman."

"This is Amos Bayler, a good friend. He is the one that found me and brought me to the hospital outside of our village. He wanted to keep me safe." She realized that she was staring at him as she spoke, and blushed.

Ms. Winter's tone softened noticeably. "Well, Mr. Bayler, you did a wonderful thing. Thank you. May I ask for a few minutes alone to speak with Mrs. Webber?"

"Sure." Amos started to stand.

"No, wait," she said to Amos. She looked at Ms. Winter. "I would like him to stay if that is possible."

Ms. Winter looked between the two f them. "Okay. Just a quick question to ask you both upfront: is this a romantic relationship? Could that be the catalyst for this situation? Not that it will make a difference. I just need to know as much as I can about the particulars."

"No, she said. Today is the first time that we have ever spoken, Ms. Winter."

"Well, okay then," she said with a smile. "Have a seat, Mr. Bayler. Let's get started and see what we can do for you, Mrs. Webber."

* * *

That night, when visiting hours were over, the nurses finally had to ask Amos to leave. He stayed until the last possible moment. And for the next two weeks, Rachel stayed in the hospital recovering from what the police had said was one of the worst beatings that they had seen in a domestic dispute in many years. During that time she was never alone. Either Amos, Samuel or her family members were there.

The day before she was leave the hospital, her mother sat in the corner chair doing needle point as Rachel read a book.

"Your bruises are looking so much better, my love," her mother said.

"My ribs are much better too. I just have to be careful when I move around."

"I want to say something to you, Rachel."

"Okay, go ahead." She was nervous about what she was going to hear, as her mother did not typically start off conversations in this manner.

"I'm so sorry." Tears pooled in her mother's eyes as she looked at her.

"Mom, what are you talking about?"

"I pushed you to marry Walter Webber. I ignored the signs that you weren't happy. I ignored the signs that you were suffering physically. I fed you with the idea that divorce is for weak, selfish women, without ever really considering how it would hurt you. I judged and I talked about things that I didn't understand. And I led you to this."

"No, mom, this is not your fault."

"We may have to agree to disagree on that point, my love." She put up her hand up as Rachel opened her mouth to argue again. "All I want to say is that I want you to divorce that monster as soon as possible. And we will help you, as will our Samuel, and your angel, Amos Bayler."

Rachel nodded, unable to speak. This was the deliverance from guilt and further suffering that she needed. Her mother understood. The community would have to understand if her mother did. She suspected that Amos had something to do with her mother's change of heart, but she didn't want to ruin the moment. Instead she decided to broach the subject that she had been avoiding for weeks. "Mom, why haven't I heard from Walter?"

Her mother gave up a sigh and shook her head. "Darling, Walter has been missing since the day that Amos brought you here to Central. The police believe that there is the possibility that foul play is involved because no one, not even his family, or his...um, friends...have heard from him."

"Mom, were going to say his girlfriend?"

Her mom looked shocked, but sighed again. "Did you know the whole time?"

"I suspected, but was too afraid to ask, for fear of his reaction."

"I'm so sorry, darling."

"Please don't. And please don't tell me who it was. I don't want to know."

Her mom nodded and said, "As you wish, my love. Let's not talk about him again for now. We can deal with this when you come home.

* * *

When Rachel returned to her community from the hospital, she decided that the best thing would be for her to return to her parents' home. The word that she received was that Walter was still missing, but she didn't want to take any chances with her safety. She was much recovered, but nowhere near strong enough to survive any abuse at his hand again. Having her mother's support and the protection of both Samuel and Amos made her feel slightly more comfortable returning to the village, but she was still scared. She had been beaten and left for dead on the floor of her own entryway. That was not something that she would soon forget.

It had not even been an hour after her return, when there was a knock at her mother's door. Rachel froze. The fear that the caller could be her husband overwhelmed her senses. Her mother quickly walked to and opened the front door. "Good afternoon." It was a man's voice, but not one that she recognized.

"Hello, how may I help you," her mother said.

"Detective John Styles of Farmington PD. I am looking for Mrs. Rachel Webber and was told that she was returning here today from Central Hospital." He spoke fast and his voice was rough with an edge of a smoker's rasp.

"I'm Rachel Webber," Rachel said loudly as she stood from her seat and made her way through the room to meet her mother at the front door. "What can I do for you, Detective?"

"I would like to speak with you about your husband, Walter Webber. May I come in?"

"Actually, why don't I come outside so that my mother can continue on with her work? There is a nice set of seats on the porch." She had no intention of letting this man into her mother's home. The community did not look favorably upon outsiders coming in to their village, and outside law enforcement, while allowed to enter and conduct business as they needed to, was not always a welcomed sight.

"Alright." He stepped back, allowing her to pass and she led him to a seat. She sat next to him and waited. "Mrs. Webber, I received a full report from the hospital about the injuries you suffered, as well as your and Mr. Bayler's versions of events. I am very sorry for your suffering."

Rachel bristled a bit at this, because he did not actually sound the least bit sorry. But she kept her comments to herself and nodded, urging him to continue.

"We have not gotten your husband's version of events."

"My understanding is that he has been missing since the day that he attacked me."

"That is no longer the case Mrs. Webber."

Her skin prickled and she spoke softly, "so you have found my husband then?"

"Yes ma'am. How long were you in the hospital?"

"Just over two weeks. Why?"

"Did you ever wonder during that time why your husband never came to see you?"

"With all due respect, Detective, if someone attacked you, would you be eager to see them again?"

"Fair point, ma'am. But that doesn't change the fact that it was strange. Was it not?"

"I just figured that he either didn't care or didn't want to deal with law enforcement outside of the village, where he is away from the community protection. What is this line of questioning about, sir?

Because I know that you have better things to do than come all the way out to the village on a muddy Tuesday afternoon to ask what I think about my husband's lack of respect for me."

The detective nodded, acknowledging her point. "Well, ma'am, it is just that we have found your husband. Or rather I should say, your husband's body."

"I'm sorry?"

"Your husband's body was discovered in the woods, off of a hiking trail early this morning. He has been dead for quite some time. We don't know the cause of death yet, but will be putting a rush on an autopsy and tox screen."

"Oh my." It was the only thing that she could will herself to say. Her head was muddled because the reality was that she was not entirely unhappy to hear the news.

"Do you know of anyone that might want to harm your husband?"

"Sorry?"

"I have been speaking to some of your neighbors, and they seem to think that your friend Samuel Wills is not a particularly big fan of your husband. Would you concur?"

"Would you like the person that was beating your best friend?"

He continued on as if he had not heard her. "And Mr. Amos Bayler. I understand that he happened upon you a few hours after the alleged assault."

"Alleged?"

"Well we do not have any witnesses beside the two of you to corroborate the stories, so I cannot place blame on an assailant at this point."

"Did you not see the pictures? I was beaten to a bloody pulp."

"Yes, Mrs. Webber. And I mean no disrespect here, but you cannot prove that your husband is the one that did that to you?"

She was stunned. He must have been kidding.

He continued on, pretending that he had not just accused a domestic assault victim of lying. "And you, Mrs. Webber, what about you?"

"What about me?"

"Yes. Did you want to hurt your husband?"

"What are you saying?"

"Well, you claim that your husband was out of control, yes?"

"Yes."

"Then, again, no disrespect, but why are you alive? From the way you describe it, he was acting as if he had no control over his behavior at that time. Why did he stop before he killed you?"

Rachel could not believe what she was hearing. There was no way that this was happening to her.

"I'm going to offer you an alternative scenario, Mrs. Webber. Perhaps you were having an affair with Mr. Amos. Perhaps you two plotted and carried out the murder of your husband and then staged a beating to make it look like he had done something horrible to you to remove suspicion. What do you think of that?"

"I think that you have been reading too many crime novels, Detective. And if you have nothing further to accuse me of, I suggest that you leave and come back with some proof or evidence supporting your wild theory."

"Fair enough. Don't' leave town, Mrs. Webber. This is not over."

After the Detective left, her mother came out the door. Her face was red and her hands were balled into fists. "So you heard that then," Rachel said. She was numb from the shock of the news and the accusation.

"I most certainly did. I am going to go speak with Samuel and Amos. You rest here, darling, and don't worry about a thing."

"Alright." She shuffled into the house and lay in her bed, not bothering to change out of her day dress. She closed her eyes and wondered vaguely, before drifting off to sleep, if this nightmare would ever end.

Over the next week, Rachel spent her time recovering at home. Her mother, Samuel and Amos, as well as other community members were all very attentive. Word had gotten around about the police accusations, and the community was standing on thin ice, waiting for the results of all of the testing.

"You need a blanket," Amos said to Rachel as they sat together on her mother's porch, one month to the day after the beating that landed her in the hospital.

"Amos, please don't fuss."

"Excuse me, Mrs. Webber?" The familiar smoker's rasp of Detective Styles drew her attention to the bottom of the porch steps.

"Hello Detective. What new theories bring you here today?" She had not meant to be rude, but her anger over the way he had treated her before was something that she wasn't capable of hiding.

Amos moved closer to her side, putting a protective hand on Rachel's shoulder. The gesture was not lost on the detective, and he continued on.

"Mrs. Webber, I and the Farmington PD would like to issue you a formal apology. Your husband drank himself into his grave. He was severely intoxicated when he died, and for whatever reason he was all the way out there, he passed out from the drink and succumbed to exposure."

"So that's it? You just issue a weak apology and expect us to trust you here in our village." Amos' voice was hard, but his touch on her should remained gentle and reassuring.

"Mr. Bayler, please believe that I am sorry for the way that the case was handled at the beginning, but I needed to be sure."

"You made a mistake and jumped the gun. I think..."

"Amos, please. Just let it go. All is fine and I don't want to think about Walter anymore. Detective, thank you for delivering the news, but now please vacate the premises and don't return to my home unless it is to save, rather than ruin someone. "

The detective looked genuinely chagrinned. He pulled some paperwork and then was on his way.

"Phew," said Amos. I was wondering when he was going to leave."

"Why?" She gasped when she looked up, as his face was right there, moving toward her. "What are you…"

But his lips were on her and his hands caressed her as if she were something sacred. She should have been scared. It should have felt awkward, but it didn't. She gave in and returned the kiss. She had a new, braver heart, born of the suffering that she had endured. In her head she thought to herself, "My new heart can now lead me to a new start. She smiled against his lips and leaned her body closer. It was time to enjoy a life without fear, suffering, or guilt. Amos had saved her life in more ways than one. Now she wanted to discover what real love could be, and she knew that she would find it with him.